What people are saying about
VORDAk THe iNcoMpRehensiBLe's
DOUBLE TROUBLE:

"The punctuation alone is worthy of a Pulitzer."
—*The Criminal Chronicle*

"And I thought *I* was bad." —*Darth Vader*

"A heartwarming tale." —*Voldemort*

"Pure nonsense." —*Commander Virtue*

"Not too bad." —*Mollie Mushnoot*

"FANTABULUTELY SPECTACULOUS!!"
—*Vordak the Incomprehensible*

"Hey! You can't blurb your own book!"
—*Mollie Mushnoot*

"Silence, you insignificant earthworm!"
—*Vordak the Incomprehensible*

"Make me!" —*Mollie Mushnoot*

ZZZRRVVAAAAAP!!!!
—*Vordak the Incomprehensible's shrink ray*

"... hey..." —*Mollie Mushnoot*

"MUAHAHAHAHA!!!"
—*Vordak the Incomprehensible*

EXTREMELY IMPORTANT!

Congratulations! By purchasing this book you have proven that you are not a complete doofus. Now don't blow it by letting it fall into the wrong hands. Fill out the information below to personalize this as your very own copy.

My last name is _____.

My first name is _____.
(But I *REALLY* wish it was _____.)

I am _____ inches tall in my bare feet.

But I am _____ inches tall when wearing my Supervillain boots.

I have _____ individual hairs on my head.
(Not including the ones in my nose)

My favorite flavor of smoothie is (circle one):

CAULIFLOWER   ASPARAGUS   SWEAT SOCK

I am pretty darn sure that the square root of 49 is _____.

On a scale of **1** to **10**, my good-lookingness rating is _____.
(with **1** being a **NAKED MOLE RAT** and **10** being **VORDAK THE INCOMPREHENSIBLE**)

There you go! Now, if anyone finds this book lying around without you next to it, they'll know exactly whom it belongs to. Only you could possibly know the answers to all of these questions about you.

Well, except for whoever finds the book and reads this page, I suppose.

Oops.

EGMONT
USA
New York

EGMONT

We bring stories to life

First published by Egmont USA, 2012
443 Park Avenue South, Suite 806
New York, NY 10016

Copyright © Scott Seegert, 2012
Illustrations by John Martin
All rights reserved

1 3 5 7 9 8 6 4 2

www.egmontusa.com
www.vordak.com

Library of Congress Cataloging-in-Publication Data
Seegert, Scott.
Double trouble / [Scott Seegert ; illustrations by John Martin].
p. cm. -- (Vordak the Incomprehensible ; #3)
Summary: Vordak clones himself in an attempt to leave behind an heir to his evil empire.
But something goes wrong when the clone is . . . nice.
ISBN 978-1-60684-372-7 (hardcover)
ISBN 978-1-60684-373-4 (e-book) [1. Supervillains--Fiction. 2. Cloning--Fiction.
3. Humorous stories.] I. Martin, John, 1963- ill. II. Title.
PZ7.S45157Do 2012
[Fic]--dc23

2012007094

Text and page layout by Karen Hudson

Printed in U.S.A.

DEDICATION

After personally dedicating my first two books to myself—and rightfully so, I might add— my publisher says I need to go with someone else this time around. So I have chosen Walter Thornscrug.

This book is dedicated to
Vordak the Incomprehensible
—Walter Thornscrug

Well done, sir!

ACKNOWLEDGMENTS

This is the section where I offer heartfelt thanks to all those individuals whose hard work, dedication and professionalism helped make this book the literary masterpiece it is. If I think of any, I'll let you know.

CHAPTER ONE

In a distant solar system many galaxies away,
a beautiful planet orbits peacefully about its life-giving sun.

For thousands of years, the planet's inhabitants have led simple lives, patiently working the land and existing peacefully with nature.

Until this fateful day.

It is Vordak the Incomprehensible, conqueror of worlds, come halfway across the universe in search of new planets to vanquish.

The victorious emperor sits high upon his throne of power, gazing down upon the vast kingdom that is now his to do with as he pleases.

The mighty beast at his side leans in close, opens its powerful jaws and...

GREAT GASSY GOBLINS, Armageddon! How many times have I told you not to wake me when I'm asleep in the Vordalounger?! That's the third time this week that a glorious victory has been cut short by a face full of slobber! Now, what in Zarnog's name is so important?

RUFF!

WHAT? ARMAGEDDON, YOU MUST SPEAK UP.

RUFF!

I STILL CAN'T . . .

RUFF!

WELL, THERE'S NO NEED TO
GET ALL SNOTTY ABOUT IT.

"maybe he needs to go outside."

Well, of *course* he needs to go outside! Do you really think I don't know that he needs to . . . Wait a minute—who are you? And how do you know that Armageddon is a he?

"I'm the reader. And I just assumed because of the mustache."

Armageddon, you've been into my Diabolical Disguise Kit again, haven't you? Now, take that mustache off this instant!

And as for you—the *reader*? Of what?

"Your book. What else?"

My book?! I haven't written another book!

"Sure you have. What do you think I'm flipping through right now? Look down below—there's a page number and everything."

By the ridiculously square chin of Commander Virtue, you're right! This is certainly strange. I don't recall writing a third book.

"Well, you did, and so far it's pretty good."

PRETTY GOOD?! I'll have you know this is one of the most stupendous pieces of literature ever written! Even if I don't remember writing it! And I'll also have you know that . . . *Just a minute, Armageddon* . . . And I'll also have you know that . . . *Stop it, Armageddon. I'm in the middle of giving this doofus a good scolding* . . . And I'll also have you know that . . . *GOOD GRIEF, Armageddon! What is it?*

ACK! Your appointment with the veterinarian! In all the commotion, I nearly forgot. Fetch me the keys and let's get a move on. You know how grouchy Doctor Venomous gets if we're late.

"can I go along?"

I have the feeling you're going to keep reading even if I say no, so I don't see how I can stop you. At least not yet. Let's go, Armageddon.

Hmm. It appears we have run into a bit of a traffic jam. I suppose we'll just have to make the best of it, Armageddon.

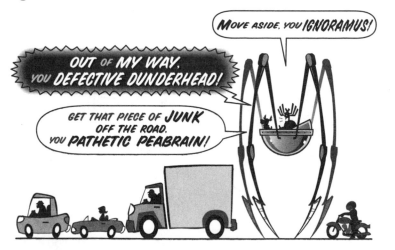

Ah, that's better. I'll admit that when I woke from my nap earlier, I wasn't in the best of moods. But there's nothing like an afternoon drive to lift one's spirits!

VINCENT VENOMOUS
VILLAINOUS VETERINARY

And look—we made it to the office with time to spare.

ACK! The only available seat is next to that bragging blowhard, the Blue Buzzard. There goes my good mood.

WELL, WELL. IF IT ISN'T
VORDAK THE INCOMPREHENSIBLE.

 WRONG AS USUAL, BUZZARD. IT *IS*
VORDAK THE INCOMPREHENSIBLE.

 AH, I SEE YOU HAVEN'T CHANGED A BIT.
AND THAT'S **BLUE** BUZZARD, MY FRIEND.
WITH A CAPITAL **B**. WHAT ARE YOU
DOING HERE?

 I BROUGHT ARMAGEDDON IN
FOR HIS CHECKUP.

 HMMM . . . FUNNY THAT YOU WOULDN'T
JUST ORDER DR. VENOMOUS TO COME
OUT TO YOUR LAIR. AFTER ALL, YOU MUST
RULE THE WORLD BY NOW, RIGHT?

 NO. NOT YET.

 OH, THAT'S TOO BAD. I KNOW
THAT'S BEEN YOUR MAIN GOAL FOR, LIKE,
YOUR **ENTIRE LIFE**, RIGHT? WELL, YOU'VE
AT LEAST CAPTURED AND DISPOSED
OF YOUR ARCH-NEMESIS, COMMANDER
VIRTUE, SINCE I'VE SEEN YOU LAST?

 I'M WORKING ON IT.

 I'M SURE YOU ARE. DID I MENTION THAT MY SON, BUZZ, WAS RECENTLY NAMED MIDDLE SCHOOL VILLAIN OF THE YEAR BY THE LEAGUE OF VILLAINOUS VILLAINY? THIS MAKES TWO YEARS IN A ROW. BY THE WAY, HOW ARE *YOUR* KIDS DOING?

 WELL, I . . .

 OH, THAT'S RIGHT—YOU DON'T *HAVE* ANY, DO YOU? THAT'S TOO BAD. I WOULD HAVE LOVED FOR YOU TO COME AND WATCH BUZZ AND ME DEFEND OUR GLORIOUS GAMES CHAMPIONSHIP AT THE ANNUAL SUPERVILLAIN AND SON PICNIC. WE'VE WON THAT ONE *THREE* YEARS IN A ROW. HERE'S A COPY OF THE FLYER WITH OUR PICTURE ON IT. THEY'VE EVEN RENAMED THE TROPHY IN OUR HONOR.

BLUE
BUZZARD & SON
MEMORIAL CUP

*WELL, IT LOOKS LIKE THE DOCTOR IS READY TO SEE US. IT WAS CERTAINLY INTERESTING CATCHING UP WITH YOU, VORDAK. PERHAPS WE'LL SEE YOU AND YOUR . . . **DOG**, IS IT? . . . AROUND TOWN.*

Oh, how I despise that bulbous-beaked blabbermouth! How can anyone be so full of himself? And he's not even brilliant or athletic or handsome like me! Come on, Armageddon, let's get out of here. It makes me nauseous just breathing the same air as that feathered fathead.

Oh, cheer up, Armageddon. I know you didn't get one of Doctor Venomous's special treats, but I'll reschedule your appointment when we return home. You know, as much as it pains me to admit it, that bird-faced boaster did have a point. I've been devising EVIL PLANS to take over the world for as long as I can remember. And I've come oh so close so many times! Remember when I seized control of the entire upper level of the Crater Valley Mall? I was well on my way to world domination that time for sure—until Commander Virtue showed up and turned all the escalators back on.

And speaking of the cauliflower-brained Commander, why *is* it that I have never been able to properly dispose of him? I've captured him dozens of times and hooked him up to all sorts of my diabolically clever yet extremely slow-acting death traps. Yet he has managed to escape *every single time*! It simply doesn't make any sense.

"maybe you're not quite as brilliant as you think you are."

BALDERDASH! I'm brilliant enough to *know* if I wasn't as brilliant as I thought I was! And I don't, so I am! There must be some other reason.

"well, ruling the world does seem pretty difficult."

Of course it's difficult! That's exactly why I want to do it! That and the fact that I would be the first one to get all the new video games when they come out.

Ah, but what's the use? Up to this point, my only successes have been in my dreams. I suppose I could sleep twenty-four hours a day. But then who would take care of Armageddon? It looks like I'm never going to rule the world. . . .

"maybe if you set your sights a bit lower, you could regain your confidence."

And maybe if you would quit bothering me, I could come up with a brilliant idea. *Wait! I just did!* Perhaps if I were to set my sights a bit lower, just for a short while . . .

"But I just said--"

Silence, you particularly unpleasant pest! You dare to interrupt me when I'm in the middle of a brilliantly brilliant brainstorm?! Yes, that's it! I will devise a far simpler Evil Plan, one that I will be able to achieve with ease. And I will build upon that success with another simple Evil Plan! And then another! And *another*! AND ANOTHER! Then, when I am once again brimming with supreme evil confidence, I will launch my Ultimate EVIL PLAN to **RULE THE WORLD!** *MUAHAHAHAHA!!!*

"What is your ultimate EVIL PLAN to rule the world?"

Ehh, I've got a whole drawer full of them. But I'll worry about that later. Right now I need a quick little Evil Plan, something to get me started. Something that will . . . GREAT GASSY GOBLINS! What's that?

"Oh, GROSS! I rubbed my hand on it! I think I'm going to be sick. I don't . . . Hey, wait a minute. It's not real."

Of course it isn't. But that sick feeling in your stomach is! Which means my Evil Plan was a success! Come on, Armageddon. That felt so good that I'm going to pull over to the curb so we can unleash a bit more evil before we return home.

By the Salty Seas of Slagnor, that felt good! Come, Armageddon. Let's get back to the lair so I can devise even more sinisterly simple acts of evil! I'll take the back way and maybe we can lose this ridiculous reader.

CHAPTER TWO

"Wait a minute. That's your 'evil lair'?
It doesn't look so evil to me."

Oh, great—you're still here! And, yes, that's sarcasm. The reason it doesn't look so evil is because the bulk of it is underground.

You certainly didn't expect me to put my top secret, hidden evil lair right out in the open now, did you?! What kind of Supervillain *are* you, anyway?

"I'm not a supervillain."

Well, I can see why! Let me take a wild guess and say you aren't even wearing black. And you don't have a cape. Or any minions. In fact, I'm willing to bet you don't even have a very intimidating evil laugh, do you?

Come on—let's hear it.

"heeheehee *snort*"

Just as I thought. I've heard more menacing sounds coming from a two-week-old bunny. I almost get the feeling you didn't even *read* my first book, *How to Grow Up and Rule the World.*

"you have another book?"

I HAVE TWO!!! Have you just recently arrived on this planet from a distant galaxy? Did you just learn how to read in the past few weeks? How in Naznor's name could you possibly not know about my magnificent works of literary genius?

"I've been reading Harry Potter."

Never heard of it. Now, I need you to pipe down. I have some simple Evil Plans to devise. Let's see now . . . I could:

1. Rearrange all the books in the library by color.
2. Hide all the toilet paper in the elementary-school bathrooms.
3. Poke holes in the milk cartons at the Shop-A-Lot.

"or you could enter the Glorious Games at the supervillain and son picnic. That Blue Buzzard was a real jerk, even for a supervillain."

Now hold on just one minute! We're not *all* jerks. Well, actually, I suppose we are. . . . But isn't that what makes us Supervillains in the first place?

Wait just a moment. All this talk of Supervillains has given me a fantastic idea for an Evil Plan! I could enter the Glorious Games at the Supervillain and Son Picnic!

"But I just--"

Quiet! I do not want to lose my evil train of thought. I could grace the picnic with my awesome presence, undoubtedly sign numerous autographs and defeat the Blue Buzzard, thereby bringing him feelings of tremendous shame, grief, self-doubt, anger, jealousy, disgust, despair, disappointment, frustration, outrage, anguish, depression, and—best of all—humiliation! He would then spend the remainder of his days cooped up inside his lair and never show his foul fowl face again! MUAHAHAHAHA!!!

It is decided, then! I shall, indeed, attend the Supervillain and Son Picnic! There are a just few minor details I need to work out:

1. I don't know when it is.
2. I don't know where it is.
3. I don't, technically, have a son.

"Well, that flyer the Buzzard gave you should help with the first two. That third one could be a problem, though."

Bah! With all the wondrous things I have accomplished during my villainous career, I certainly don't think the lack of a son can stop me from competing at a Supervillain and Son Picnic!

"What?"

I said with all the wondrous things—

"No. What wondrous things have you accomplished during your career?"

Oh, lots of things. Tons of things. *Oodles and oodles* of things. It would take far too long to mention them all right now.

"I'm not busy."

Of course you're not. But I am, so let's move along. As I was saying, with all the wondrous things I have accomplished during my villainous career, I certainly don't think I'll have much trouble coming up with a son. In fact, while you were reading that last sentence, *I already did.*

On second thought, that will never work. Every Supervillain at the picnic will have used robots at some point during their own attempts to take over the world. They'll sniff out my deception from a mile away. My son is going to have to be an actual living, breathing being. If I could only . . . *OF COURSE*! What an ingenious idea! Why didn't I think of this sooner?! The answer has been sitting (and scratching) right in front of me the entire time!

Hmmm. No offense, Armageddon, but now that I take a good look at you, no one would believe for one minute that someone as spectacular looking as I could possibly have a son who looks like . . . well, you. Oh, what's the point? Where will I ever find someone deserving of being the son of Vordak the Incomprehensible? Such a person simply does not exist.

"You could always clone yourself."

Wait a moment. . . . A brilliant thought just crept into my brain. . . .

"Hey, you're not going to steal my idea agai--"

QUIET! The thought is twisting and swirling around in my mind, slowly taking shape and becoming clearer as I increase my concentration. I just about have it . . . almost there . . . *GOT IT!* You, the reader, will be my son! If you're a girl, we'll just give you a short haircut and remove your nail polish! It's a brilliant idea! A positively remarkable . . . *HEY, WAIT A MINUTE!* What am I thinking? You can't be my son—you're an ignoramus! That can't be my brilliant idea. Let me re-concentrate and try this again.

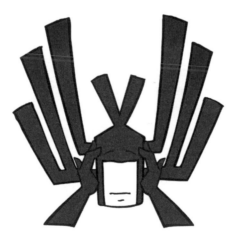

Concentrating . . . concentrating . . . (*well, come on*) . . . concentrating . . . (*what are you waiting for?*) . . . concentrating . . .

"oh, for crying out loud.
I said you could always clone yourself."

I HAVE IT! I will *clone* myself! I mean, when you get right down to it, who else could possibly be worthy of being my son besides . . . ME?! Imagine: two Vordak the Incomprehensibles. Double the brilliance. Double the evil. Double the good looks. Myself and I would be unstoppable! First the picnic, and then . . . THE WORLD! MUAHAHAHAHA!!!

I'm going to require some help with this one, though. Sure, I have cloned minions for my armies in the past, but I didn't really care if those turned out right or not since they're only minions. Minions are a dime a dozen. And they certainly aren't very bright. All they basically need to be able to do is terrorize the countryside in large numbers. And follow the simplest of orders. And wash my evil undies. Say, you may not have what it takes to be my son, but you would make an *excellent* minion! What do you say?

■ ■ ■ ■ ■ ■ ■ ■ ■ ■ ■ ■

Well, that seems to have shut you up. Now, as I was saying, I must find myself an expert cloning scientist to help ensure nothing goes wrong. I shall create an advertisement and use my highly advanced equipment and technical know-how to spread it across the globe via the Internet! MUAHAHAHAHA!!!

What's that, Armageddon? Our computer has a virus? No matter—I'll just go with plan B.

HELP WANTED

clone scientist to serve as toady to world-renowned supervillain. Experience cloning very good-looking individuals a plus. Must have proof as to your cloning abilities. Contact V the I, whereabouts unknown.

There. Nothing to do now but sit back and wait for a knock at the door.

knock knock

Well, it's about time!

 HELLO. I'M HERE REGARDING YOUR AD.

 ACK! CAN'T YOU READ? THE AD CLEARLY SAID "CLONE" SCIENTIST. CLONE!

 I AM A CLONE SCIENTIST.

 THEN WHAT'S WITH THE RIDICULOUS GETUP?

 OH, THIS? I WAS ON MY WAY HOME FROM WORKING A PRESCHOOL BIRTHDAY PARTY WHEN I SAW YOUR ADVERTISEMENT NAILED TO A TELEPHONE POLE. THERE AREN'T A LOT OF OPPORTUNITIES IN CLONING RIGHT NOW AND A GUY HAS TO MAKE A LIVING, YOU KNOW?

I SUPPOSE.

THE AD SAYS THAT YOU'RE A SUPERVILLAIN. DOES THAT MEAN YOU'RE EVIL?

 DIABOLICALLY SO! IS THAT A PROBLEM?

NO, I SUPPOSE NOT. IT'S JUST THAT, UP UNTIL NOW, ALL MY CLONING WORK HAS BEEN DONE FOR THE POWERS OF GOOD. MAY I ASK WHAT THE JOB PAYS?

 IT PAYS NOTHING! BUT IF YOUR WORK IS SATISFACTORY, I MAY DECIDE **NOT** TO THROW YOU INTO A VAT OF BOILING YOGURT.

HMMM. THAT SOUNDS A **LOT** BETTER THAN THESE BIRTHDAY GIGS. I'LL TAKE IT!

 NOT SO FAST, YOU BOULDER-NOSED BUMPKIN! I WILL DECIDE WHETHER YOU ARE WORTHY OF MY EMPLOY OR NOT. WHAT PROOF DO YOU HAVE AS TO YOUR CLONING ABILITIES?

 **IMPRESSIVE. BUT HOW DO I KNOW YOU AREN'T MERELY TWINS?**

WELL, FOR ONE THING, WE BOTH HAVE THE EXACT SAME WART ON OUR REAR ENDS. WANT TO SEE?

 **NOT UNDER ANY CIRCUMSTANCES.**

AND, SINCE OUR MINDS ARE EXACTLY THE SAME, WE THINK EXACTLY THE SAME AND SAY THE EXACT SAME THING AT THE EXACT SAME TIME.

SO I NOTICED. WELL, THIS IS YOUR LUCKY DAY. I DON'T HAVE TIME TO INTERVIEW ANY OTHER CANDIDATES, SO THE JOB IS YOURS. BE HERE BRIGHT AND EARLY AT 11:30 TOMORROW MORNING AND WE'LL GET STARTED. AND WIPE THOSE RIDICULOUS SMILES OFF YOUR FACES! YOU'RE SUPPOSED TO BE EVIL, FOR GORZAK'S SAKE!

11:29 the next morning . . .

knock knock

ACK! How dare you show up early! I was right in the middle of another spectacular dream about conquering—

GREAT GASSY GOBLINS! MY AD CLEARLY STATED THAT YOU NEEDED EXPERIENCE CLONING **GOOD-LOOKING** INDIVIDUALS.

WELL, THAT'S JUST PLAIN MEAN.

GET USED TO IT! I'M EVIL, REMEMBER?! AND WHY ARE YOU **BOTH** HERE? I ONLY REQUIRE ONE CLONING SCIENTIST.

WE COULDN'T DECIDE WHO SHOULD COME. BESIDES, OUR BIRTHDAY PARTY ACT IS DESIGNED FOR A DUO, SO THE OTHER ONE OF US WOULDN'T HAVE ANYTHING TO DO, ANYWAY.

OH, VERY WELL. I'LL JUST HAVE TO REMEMBER TO ORDER MORE YOGURT TO BOIL. BY THE WAY, I WILL NEED TO KNOW WHAT TO CALL YOU SO I CAN MOCK AND THREATEN YOU EFFECTIVELY. WHAT ARE YOUR NAMES?

FRED.

WHAT ABOUT THE OTHER ONE?

WE'RE BOTH NAMED FRED. THAT'S HOW CLONING WORKS.

 ACK! ALREADY YOU TEST MY PATIENCE! ARMAGEDDON, TAKE THE FREDS DOWN TO THE LABORATORY. AND TURN UP THE TEMPERATURE IN THE YOGURT VAT.

CHAPTER THREE

I have given the Freds twenty-four hours to complete my Cloning Chamber. Hopefully they are a bit brighter than my last brainiac, Professor Cranium.

"Who's he?"

Well, where have you been?

"I had to go to the bathroom. Who's Professor Cranium?"

Hmmm. Apparently you didn't read my second book, *Rule the School*, either. I brought Cranium on board to develop my Fantastically Frigid Freeze Ray, which I intended to use to conquer the planet. Unfortunately, he was a bit of a doofus and . . . well, it would take far too long to recount the tale right now.

"I'm not busy."

Yes. We have already established that fact. But, since I'm not here to entertain you, you'll just have to read the book. And why is it that you never seem to be busy? Don't you have studying or chores or your grandmother's toenails to trim or *something* to occupy your time?

"Actually, I AM studying. I'm using this book to help me with my science class."

Brilliant! Unlike other textbooks, *my* books contain nothing but facts. Brilliant, invaluably villainous facts! And, also unlike other textbooks, mine has an extremely handsome author photo in the back.

Ah, Armageddon! The Freds' twenty-four hours are nearly up! In a few moments there will be either cloning or boiling yogurt screams to entertain us! Let's take you outside while we have the chance.

Well, Armageddon, it looks like we have some new neighbors to ignore. Someone finally bought that house across the street. Suckers. It doesn't even have a secret underground lair or a missile silo or anything.

At last! The timer has reached zero! That means twenty-four hours have passed and my Calamitous Cloning Chamber finally should be complete! I can hardly contain my excitement! Come, Armageddon. Let's head down to the laboratory.

 *BY THE CHUBBY CHINS OF CHORVATH! THERE ARE **THREE** OF YOU NOW?!*

WE HAD TO TEST THE CHAMBER. AND, ACTUALLY, IT'S FOUR. FRED HAD TO USE THE RESTROOM. HE'LL BE BACK IN A MINUTE.

 WELL, EVERYTHING APPEARS TO BE IN ORDER. SET THE BEAM TO CREATE A TWELVE-YEAR-OLD CLONE OF MYSELF AT ONCE! TIME IS OF THE ESSENCE!

THAT'S IT? NO PATS ON THE BACKS? NO "JOB WELL DONE"? NOT EVEN A "THANK YOU"?

HA! IT'S OBVIOUS THIS IS YOUR FIRST TIME SERVING UNDER THE HAND OF A SUPERVILLAIN. NOW EITHER PREPARE THE CHAMBER OR PREPARE TO BE YOGURTED!

OKAY, OKAY. SHEESH, WHAT A GROUCH.

BY THE BULGING BUTTOCKS OF BRANDOR, WHAT HAVE YOU DONE?

CREATED A 112-YEAR-OLD CLONE OF YOU, JUST AS YOU ASKED.

ALL RIGHT, FIRST OFF, VORDAK THE INCOMPREHENSIBLE DOESN'T **ASK**—HE **DEMANDS**. AND, SECOND OFF, I SAID **TWELVE** YEARS OLD, YOU FOURSOME OF FECKLESS FATHEADS! **TWELVE!** WHAT POSSIBLE REASON COULD I HAVE FOR CLONING A 112-YEAR-OLD VERSION OF MYSELF?

TREATS FOR YOUR DOG?

 ACK! PUT ME DOWN THIS INSTANT, ARMAGEDDON! AND DON'T EVEN *THINK* OF BURYING ME IN THE BACKYARD. AS FOR YOU, YOU QUARTET OF INCOMPETENT QUACKS . . .

QUINTET.

 WHAT?!

THERE WAS A SMALL LEAK IN THE CLONING CHAMBER AND FRED HERE WAS STANDING A BIT TOO CLOSE, SO . . .

 ENOUGH! LET ME GO OVER THIS ONE MORE TIME SO THAT EVEN YOU CAN UNDERSTAND. I REQUIRE A TWELVE-YEAR-OLD ME SO THAT I, ALONG WITH MYSELF, CAN ENTER THE GLORIOUS GAMES AT THE SUPERVILLAIN AND SON PICNIC. IS THAT CLEAR?!

OH, ABSOLUTELY.

 WELL THEN! REVISE THE CHAMBER'S SETTINGS AND GET ON WITH IT! I DON'T HAVE ALL DAY!

IT WORKED! And just look at me! What a remarkable, good-looking, brilliant, diabolically evil young man I was . . . err . . . *am*. With me at my side, there is nothing I . . . err . . . *we* cannot accomplish. Why, Commander Virtue himself will have no choice but to succumb to me . . . err . . . *us*. ACK! This is all so confusing.

WHO IS COMMANDER VIRTUE?

 WHAT?! BY THE PURPLE PIMPLES OF PLORZAK, FREDS—YOU HAVE FAILED ME AGAIN! A TRUE CLONE OF VORDAK THE INCOMPREHENSIBLE WOULD SURELY KNOW WHO HIS VERY OWN HATED ARCH-NEMESIS IS! FREDS, PREPARE YOURSELVES TO BE DIPPED IN BOILING YOGURT—IN SHIFTS, OF COURSE. MY YOGURT VAT HAS A MAXIMUM OCCUPANCY OF TWO.

WAIT! WE DID NOT FAIL. YOUR CLONE ONLY KNOWS WHAT YOU KNEW AT AGE TWELVE AND NOTHING MORE. DO YOU KNOW **ANYTHING** ABOUT CLONING?

HA! DO I KNOW ANYTHING ABOUT CLONING? IS *EVERYTHING* ANYTHING? BECAUSE ANYTHING IS *NOTHING* TO EVERYTHING I KNOW ABOUT CLONING.

IS THAT CLEAR?

OH, ABSOLUTELY.

GOOD. NOW, I WILL DETERMINE WHETHER THIS CLONE IS TRULY ME BY ASKING A FEW QUESTIONS ABOUT EVENTS FROM MY YOUTH THAT I AND I ALONE KNOW THE ANSWERS TO. WHAT IS MY FAVORITE COLOR?

BLACK.

ACK! THESE ARE QUESTIONS FOR ME . . . ERR . . . MY CLONE!

WELL, YOU HAD BETTER MAKE THEM A BIT HARDER. THAT ONE WAS PRETTY OBVIOUS, AND WE'VE ONLY KNOWN YOU FOR A COUPLE OF DAYS.

VERY WELL. ANSWER ME THIS, YOUNG ME: WHERE DID I GO TO—

L. LEMENTARY ELEMENTARY.

AND WHO WAS MY—

MISS CRUDDUZZLE.

HOW MANY TIMES DID I—

5,762.

OKAY, LAST QUESTION:
WHAT DID I PUT IN SUZIE
LUMPKIN'S—

A LUMBRICUS TERRESTRIS—

NO! IT WAS A—

—OR COMMON EARTHWORM.

GREAT GASSY GOBLINS, it *is* me! And not a moment too soon—the picnic is tomorrow! Let's go, young me. You're going to need a good night's sleep.

CHAPTER FOUR

Ah, what a glorious morning! A mild breeze is blowing, the sun is shining, and the scent of another Vordak victory is in the air!

Well, well. It appears our new neighbors are installing a satellite dish, Armageddon. I must remember to tap into their signal when it is complete. There is nothing quite like the thrill of watching Cartoon Network for free! MUAHAHAHAHA!!! But I have more immediate concerns. It's time to wake my younger self.

Rise and shine, you handsome young villain, you. The picnic beckons. I can't wait to see the look on Buzzard's face when me and I show up. I remember being quite the athlete when I was younger, so I'm expecting a lot out of you, Vordy.

MY NAME IS VORDAK THE INCOMPREHENSIBLE.

WELL, OBVIOUSLY. BUT THAT'S GOING TO BE A BIT CONFUSING, SO I THOUGHT WE WOULD CALL YOU VORDY.

OR, HOW ABOUT THIS— IN ORDER TO AVOID CONFUSION, WE'LL CALL *YOU* VORDY.

WHY, THAT'S PREPOSTEROUS! I AM *VORDAK THE INCOMPREHENSIBLE!*

SO AM I. WHAT MAKES YOU THINK YOU'RE ANY MORE INCOMPREHENSIBLE THAN I AM?

WELL, FOR ONE THING, I'M A LOT OLDER THAN YOU!

YEAH, ABOUT THAT. WHAT HAPPENED? I WAS SORT OF EXPECTING TO BE A LOT BETTER LOOKING WHEN I GREW UP. AND IN WAY BETTER SHAPE.

WHAT?! YOU HAVE A LOT OF NERVE! BUT I GUESS I ALREADY KNEW THAT, BECAUSE I HAVE A LOT OF NERVE. ALL RIGHT, LOOK—WE'LL BOTH BE VORDAK THE INCOMPREHENSIBLE. THE IMPORTANT THING IS TO GET TO THE PICNIC IN TIME TO TAKE THAT TROPHY FROM THE BUZZARD! BUT FIRST, LET ME EXPLAIN HOW CHEESE IS MADE.

"Excuse me?"

Ah, good, you're still here. I wouldn't want you to miss this. The making of a quality cheese begins with quality milk, which must be weighed and pasteurized to ensure a safe, uniform cheese product. Bacteria is then added to the milk to begin the cheese-making process. Next, an enzyme called rennet is added to . . . Hello? Hello, reader . . . are you still there?

"zzzzzzzzzzzzzzzzzzzzzz"

Yes! I knew no one could possibly stay awake through that bombastically boring cheese blathering! As long as we leave quietly, that reader should stay asleep until we return from the picnic. That should teach them to be a little more respectful of Vordak the Incomprehensible! Come on, Vordy . . . err . . . Vordak. Let's get a move on. I'll explain everything on the way.

Blah blah blah Supervillain and Son Picnic *blah blah blah* Cloning Chamber *blah blah blah* a whole bunch of Freds *blah blah blah* pretend you are my son *blah blah blah* win trophy from stupid Buzzard and his dimwitted kid *blah blah blah* conquer the planet *blah blah blah* rent *Transformers* DVD *blah blah blah*.

At last! We have arrived!

Oops! Wrong picnic! Ours must be farther up the road.

Ah, here we go.

VORDAK? WHAT A SURPRISE TO SEE *YOU* HERE. CAME TO WATCH BUZZ AND ME WIN ANOTHER GLORIOUS GAMES CHAMPIONSHIP, EH?

ACTUALLY, BUZZARD, I'M GOING TO WIN THAT TROPHY MYSELF.

YOU? I'M SO SORRY, VORDAK, BUT AS I EXPLAINED, THIS IS A COMPETITION FOR SUPERVILLAINS AND THEIR **SONS**.

SPEAKING OF WHICH, I'D LIKE YOU TO MEET MY CLONE . . . ERR . . . **SON**, VORDY.

WHAT? SINCE WHEN DO *YOU* HAVE A SON?

 SINCE **YESTERDAY**, YOU WINGED WINDBAG. ERR . . . THAT IS TO SAY, VORDY RETURNED HOME FROM BOARDING SCHOOL YESTERDAY, SO WE DECIDED TO SHOW UP AND WIN YOUR MISERABLE LITTLE TROPHY.

YOU KNOW, IT'S FUNNY YOU'VE NEVER MENTIONED THAT YOU HAD A SON BEFORE.

 WELL, YOU KNOW ME, BUZZARD. I HATE TO BRAG—EVEN THOUGH I WOULD BE THE BEST BRAGGER ON THE PLANET IF I DID. SO, WHEN DO THESE "GAMES" BEGIN?

OH, IN ABOUT FIFTEEN MINUTES. THE SIGN-UP SHEET IS RIGHT OVER THERE.

— LOST —
BASEBALL - SIZED CLUMP OF KRYPTONITE
CONTACT LEX LUTHOR FOR REWARD
555-78

Glorious Games
- Savage sack race relay
- Terrifying tetherball
- Sinister Slimon Says
- Spectacular spoon and egg relay
- Horrible hot dog eating contest

Sign up:

Blue Buzzard

BUZZ

FACE PAINTING
TODAY FROM 2-3pm
PRESENTED BY THE JOKER

WAIT A MINUTE! NOBODY ELSE HAS ENTERED THE CONTEST BUT YOU.

WELL, CAN YOU BLAME THEM? AFTER ALL, BUZZ AND I ARE THE THREE-TIME DEFENDING CHAMPIONS.

NO ONE HAS THE COURAGE TO CHALLENGE US.

NO WAY! THAT THING IS *SOOOOO* LAME. LET'S PLAY VOLLEYBALL.

MAYBE WE SHOULD SIGN UP FOR THE GLORIOUS GAMES THIS YEAR, SON.

All the better. Now we only have to worry about that chinless chowderhead and his slow-witted son. Remember, my secondary self, that we need to win three of the five events to capture that treasured trophy. And we'll do so by following . . .

VORDAK THE INCOMPREHENSIBLE'S
Carefully Constructed Creed of Competitive Conduct

1. Always respect your opponent.

2. Always follow the rules.

3. Always display good sportsmanship.

4. Unless it looks like you are going to lose—then resort to any level of treachery necessary to ensure victory! MUAHAHAHAHA!!!

Ack! We only have a few minutes until the contest begins! I had better loosen up.

Jab *and* Stretch *and* Bend *and* Out

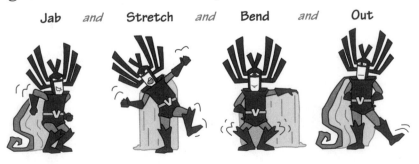

They're calling us over now. Time to show that nest making namby-pamby who the *real* Supervillain is around here.

ALL RIGHT, WE'RE TIED AT TWO EVENTS APIECE. I MUST SAY, I REMEMBER BEING A MUCH BETTER TETHERBALL PLAYER WHEN I WAS YOUR AGE.

WELL, IT SURE DOESN'T LOOK LIKE I'M GOING TO IMPROVE MUCH AS I GET OLDER, EITHER.

HEY, I ALREADY TOLD YOU— THE SUN WAS IN MY EYES! AND THE GROUND WAS SLIPPERY! AND THE BALL WASN'T INFLATED PROPERLY! AND I FORGOT TO BRING MY TETHERBALL GLOVES! ACK! IT DOESN'T MATTER. WE JUST NEED TO WIN THE HOT DOG EATING CONTEST AND WE WILL HAVE THE GREATEST, MOST GLORIOUS VICTORY OF OUR LIFE!

WAIT A MINUTE. THIS IS THE MOST WE'VE ACCOMPLISHED IN OUR ENTIRE LIFE?

WELL, TECHNICALLY SPEAKING . . . YES. OH, I'VE COME PAINFULLY CLOSE TO TRULY DIABOLICAL GREATNESS A NUMBER OF TIMES. BUT THAT MUSCLE-MOUTHED MEATHEAD COMMANDER VIRTUE ALWAYS SWOOPS IN AT THE LAST MINUTE AND THWARTS MY PLANS. ZOUNDS, I DISLIKE THAT GUY! ENOUGH OF THIS, THOUGH—THEY'RE WAVING US OVER TO THE HOT DOG TABLE.

BY THE BLOATED BELLY OF BLURNAK! WE LOST! But how?! I must have eaten twenty-seven hot dogs *myself*, for Glarnog's sake! I demand a recount! I demand a video review. I demand a trash can!

YOU KNOW, VORDY, YOU DON'T APPEAR TO BE VERY FULL. HOW MANY HOT DOGS DID *YOU* EAT?

ALMOST A WHOLE ONE. BUT I DON'T THINK THEY GAVE ME CREDIT FOR IT.

ALMOST ONE?! BY THE GNARLY NOSTRIL HAIR OF NORMOOTH, I COULD EAT AT LEAST FOUR OR FIVE WHEN I WAS YOUR AGE!

WHAT CAN I SAY? I WASN'T VERY HUNGRY.

IT'S NOT ABOUT BEING HUNGRY! IT'S ABOUT JAMMING ENOUGH HOT DOGS INTO YOUR FACE TO TAKE FIRST PLACE! IF I DIDN'T KNOW BETTER, I WOULD ALMOST THINK YOU DIDN'T CARE ABOUT WINNING!

WELL, TO BE HONEST . . .

 HONEST?! SINCE WHEN HAS VORDAK THE INCOMPREHENSIBLE EVER BEEN HONEST?!

. . . BEING THE GLORIOUS GAMES CHAMPIONS JUST SEEMED TO MEAN SO MUCH TO THE BLUE BUZZARD, I DIDN'T HAVE THE HEART TO TAKE THAT AWAY FROM HIM.

 DON'T YOU THINK IT MEANT A LOT TO ME?! DID I NOT MAKE MYSELF CLEAR THAT THIS WOULD BE MY . . . *OUR* . . . GREATEST VICTORY?! DID I NOT MAKE MYSELF CLEAR THAT I DESPISE THAT FLEA-BITTEN BUZZARD BEYOND DESCRIPTION?! *DID I NOT?!*

SURE YOU DID. BUT I WAS TALKING TO BUZZ AND HE SAID HIS DAD WAS GOING THROUGH SOME TOUGH TIMES LATELY, AND THIS CHAMPIONSHIP IS PRETTY MUCH ALL HE HAS. IT WOULD HAVE CRUSHED HIM TO LOSE. YOU SHOULD BE HAPPY—LETTING HIM WIN WAS THE DECENT THING TO DO.

 OF COURSE HE TOLD YOU THAT! HE'S A SUPERVILLAIN, FOR CRYING OUT LOUD! HE'LL DO ANYTHING TO WIN!

ACK! ALL THIS TALK OF "BEING HAPPY" AND "DOING THE DECENT THING"—IF I HADN'T SEEN THE PROCESS WITH MY OWN EYES, I WOULDN'T BELIEVE YOU COULD POSSIBLY BE *MY* CLONE. IT DOESN'T EVEN . . . *HEY* . . . WHERE DID YOU GO?

GREAT GASSY GOBLINS!

CHAPTER FIVE

I knew I should never have let those cloning clowns through the front door. You try your best, put a brilliant advertisement on a telephone pole, and still wind up with ignoramuses. I would have been better off using a Xerox machine.

"Hey! Where have you been? Last thing I remember, you were droning on about cheese."

We were at the Supervillain and Son Picnic.

"Really? Where's the trophy?"

Somewhere deep within the Nest Lair of the Blue Buzzard, thanks to our little clone here.

"You mean Vordak?"

Ha! Hardly. I don't know who he is a clone of, but it certainly isn't Vordak the Incomprehensible. Speaking of which, where are those full-out failures, the Freds?

 REALLY? IT'S SIX NOW?

*YEAH, SORRY ABOUT THAT.
WE WERE PLAYING HIDE-AND-SEEK,
AND FRED HERE DECIDED TO HIDE IN
THE CLONING TUBE. ONE THING LED TO
ANOTHER AND, WELL, MEET FRED.*

HOW DO YOU DO?

 *FINE, THANKS. HOW ABOUT
YOURSELF . . . **ACK!** YOU HAVE
FAILED ME FOR THE FINAL TIME!
I COMMAND ALL FREDS TO REPORT
TO THE BOILING-YOGURT VAT
IMMEDIATELY!*

ME, TOO? BUT I JUST GOT HERE.

YES, YOU, TOO. AND TAKE THAT IMPOSTER CLONE WITH YOU.

HOLD ON A MINUTE. YOU SAID THE *FINAL* TIME. THAT IMPLIES WE FAILED YOU BEFORE. WHEN WAS THAT?

WHEN YOU MADE MY 112-YEAR-OLD CLONE. I'M SURE YOU REMEMBER.

THAT WAS REALLY MORE A MISUNDERSTANDING THAN A FAILURE, DON'T YOU THINK?

I AM VORDAK THE INCOMPREHENSIBLE! I *NEVER* THINK! NOW MOVE ALONG BEFORE THE YOGURT GETS COLD!

HEY, WAIT A SECOND. EVEN COUNTING THE AGED CLONE AS A FAILURE, THAT'S ONLY ONE. WHAT'S THE *FINAL* FAILURE? AND WHAT DID YOU MEAN BY "IMPOSTER CLONE"?

THIS YOUNG CLONE OF MYSELF IS CLEARLY *NOT A YOUNG CLONE OF MYSELF!* HE'S *NICE*, FOR MOLDAF'S SAKE!

OH NO, HE'S YOUR CLONE, ALL RIGHT. HOW ELSE WOULD HE HAVE KNOWN THE ANSWERS TO ALL THOSE PERSONAL QUESTIONS YOU ASKED? AND LOOK AT HIM COMPARED TO THIS PHOTO OF YOU TAKEN WHEN YOU WERE THAT SAME AGE. YOU'RE IDENTICAL.

HA! THIS MERELY SERVES TO PROVE MY POINT! MY SMILE IS DIABOLICAL. HIS IS . . . NOT. AND THAT IS DEFINITELY **NOT** A POISONOUS SERPENT HE'S HOLDING. ADMIT IT, YOU SORRY SEXTET OF SIMPLETONS— YOU GOOFED! THE SIX OF YOU COMBINED DON'T EQUAL THE BRAINPOWER OF A HERMIT CRAB.

IF YOU HAVE ANY DOUBTS, WE CAN RUN A DNA TEST ON THE TWO OF YOU THAT WOULD ABSOLUTELY, POSITIVELY DETERMINE WHETHER HE IS YOUR CLONE OR NOT.

WELL, WHY DIDN'T YOU MENTION THAT EARLIER? LET'S DO IT.

IT WILL INVOLVE BEING POKED WITH A NEEDLE.

LET'S NOT DO IT.

LOOK, YOUR AWESOMENESS, APPARENTLY YOU HAVE AT LEAST SOME TINY MORSEL OF GOODNESS SOMEWHERE DEEP DOWN INSIDE. WHEN WE CLONED YOU, YOUR NEW SELF MUST HAVE LATCHED ON TO THAT MORSEL AND DECIDED TO BE GOOD RATHER THAN EVIL. IT HAPPENS.

NOT TO ME IT DOESN'T! THAT'S ABSURD.

NOT REALLY. IN FACT, THERE IS A GOOD CHANCE THAT THE ONLY REASON YOU'RE EVEN EVIL IN THE FIRST PLACE IS BECAUSE YOUR FATHER WAS A VILLAIN AND YOUR PARENTS RAISED YOU IN A HIGHLY VILLAINOUS MANNER.

WHY, THAT'S RIDICULOUS! OUTRAGEOUS! PREPOSTREOU . . . PROPESTEROU . . .

PREPOSTEROUS?

EXACTLY! THE VERY IDEA THAT VORDAK THE INCOMPREHENSIBLE IS NOT DIABOLICALLY EVIL RIGHT THROUGH TO HIS ABOMINABLE BLOOD CELLS IS DOWNRIGHT . . . INCOMPREHENSIBLE!

EVIL
(99.9999%)

GOOD
(0.0001%)

On the other hand, what if the six Freds are right? What if I really *do* have some tiny trace of goodness hidden somewhere deep inside me?

It *would* help to explain a few things. Such as why, as brilliant as I am, I have never ever ever been able to RULE THE WORLD! Perhaps that teensy-weensy tiny morsel of goodness is sabotaging everything I do. What other reason could there possibly be? Besides the sun being in my eyes, I mean.

And then there is Commander Virtue. I have captured him thirty-seven separate times and dropped him into all sorts of my diabolically clever yet extremely slow-acting death traps. Yet he has managed to escape *every single time*! How can that possibly be? And, now that I think of it, why do I make my death traps so darned slow-acting in the first place?

It's almost as if, deep down, I *want* him to escape. How else to explain the stupid placement of on/off levers and the "Easy Escape" ankle and wrist shackles I use? What other explanation for my failing to throw all the Freds into the boiling-yogurt vat, regardless of whether they deserved it or not? In fact, why even *use* yogurt when sulfuric acid would obviously be the more evil choice? GREAT GASSY GOBLINS! What if, way deep down inside, I really am . . . *good?!*

"I don't know about that. You've been pretty mean to me."

Well, what in Kraglor's name do you expect? You can be an incredibly annoying little troglodyte. But I let you stick around anyway, didn't I?

"YOU PUT ME TO SLEEP WITH A LECTURE ABOUT CHEESE AND THEN DITCHED ME TO GO TO THE PICNIC!"

Ah, yes—that *was* pretty darn evil! But it's no use trying to cheer me up. If I really do have a gooey glob of goodness in me somewhere, I'm going to have to get rid of it as soon as possible. It's the only way I'll ever defeat that cow-kissing Commander and RULE THE WORLD! MUAHAHAha . . . Oh, what's the use? My heart's just not in it.

CHAPTER SIX

ACK! This talk of me not being 100 percent evil is nonsense. And I'm going to prove it! I will head down to the Shop-A-Lot on the corner with my Wondrous Worm Inserter and ruin all the apples in the produce department! MUAHAHAHAHA!!!

Clearly, only the evilest of evil evildoers would even

WONDROUS WORM INSERTER

① Insert worm

② push plunger

③ Ta-Dah!
Burp!

dare *attempt* such a decidedly diabolical deed! I will return shortly. Don't touch anything while I'm gone!

"can I go?"

I suppose so, since I don't feel like discussing the production of dairy products at the moment. Don't get too excited, though—it's just up the block.

Ah, the new neighbor's satellite dish installation seems to be moving right along.

"Are you sure that's a satellite dish?"

Of course I'm sure! What else would it be? A death ray? I am the only Supervillain in the neighborhood, for Drogmyr's sake. Now pipe down— we have arrived. Ready yourself to witness evil as only Vordak the Incomprehensible can serve it up! MUAHAHAHAHA!!!

"Wow. That was impressive. Don't the Boy Scouts give merit badges for that kind of thing?"

All right, that clearly was NOT my fault! That doggone old woman caught me by surprise! And one of the worms crawled into my tights! And the sun was in my eyes! And I had to go to the bathroom! So that didn't prove a darned thing! I don't feel so good. I think I need to go lie down for a while.

A while later . . .

There, that's much better. I was obviously too tired to think clearly back at the grocery store. Now, it seems to me that if I have any good in me whatsoever, it surely would have shown up when I was younger. Freds, look up the e-mail address for my seventh-grade teacher, Miss Shmortley.

BUT WE'RE CLONING SCIENTISTS. CAN'T YOU HAVE SOMEONE ELSE DO IT?

OH, ABSOLUTELY. WHAT WAS I THINKING? GENIUSES SUCH AS YOURSELVES ARE CERTAINLY ABOVE MENIAL TASKS SUCH AS FINDING AN E-MAIL ADDRESS. I JUST ASSUMED THAT, AS CLONING SCIENTISTS WITH NO MORE CLONING TO DO, YOU WOULD PREFER THAT TO THE WHOLE BOILING-IN-YOGURT THING.

SHMORTLEY, YOU SAY? WE'LL HAVE THAT FOR YOU IN ONE SECOND, YOUR ALMOST COMPLETELY EVILNESS!

SECOND, SHMECOND! HAND OVER THAT E-MAIL ADDRESS NOW, YOU GAGGLE OF GOOFY GRINNING GASBAGS!

WHAT WAS THAT?!

OH, THAT'S JUST FRED OVER THERE CLEANING THE CLONING CHAMBER.

SORRY. I HIT THE POWER LEVER BY MISTAKE.

 **ANOTHER ONE?!
HOW MANY IS THAT, NOW?**

**LET'S SEE . . . COUNTING
FRED HERE, THAT MAKES SEVEN.**

 **OH, FOR THE LOVE OF LARDOX, JUST
GIVE ME THE E-MAIL ADDRESS!**

Shmortley was my seventh-grade teacher back in Gomersborough, Wisconsin. She tried to have me kicked out of school at least sixty-seven times that year alone. I'm sure that if I did so much as *one good thing* that year, she would have remembered.

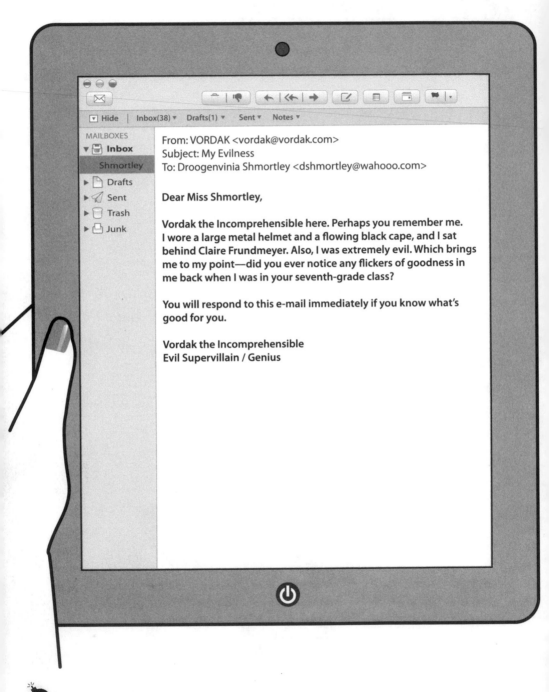

From: VORDAK <vordak@vordak.com>
Subject: My Evilness
To: Droogenvinia Shmortley <dshmortley@wahooo.com>

Dear Miss Shmortley,

Vordak the Incomprehensible here. Perhaps you remember me. I wore a large metal helmet and a flowing black cape, and I sat behind Claire Frundmeyer. Also, I was extremely evil. Which brings me to my point—did you ever notice any flickers of goodness in me back when I was in your seventh-grade class?

You will respond to this e-mail immediately if you know what's good for you.

Vordak the Incomprehensible
Evil Supervillain / Genius

From: Droogenvinia Shmortley <dshmortley@wahooo.com>
Subject: RE: My Evilness
To: VORDAK <vordak@vordak.com>

Vordak,

Do I remember you? You are the reason we no longer serve pudding in the school cafeteria. Or keep caterpillars in the classroom. Or play dodgeball at recess. Or allow papier-mâché volcanoes in the science fair. Or bring in cupcakes on birthdays. Or have show-and-tell. Or go on field trips. And we're still trying to get Carl Spaldek's underwear down from the flagpole.

It doesn't surprise me one bit that you became an Evil Supervillain, Genius, on the other hand, I find difficult to believe.

As for whether I remember you ever doing anything good, off the top of my head I would have to say . . . NO. Not one single thing. And, speaking of "off the top of my head," I'm sure it will please you to know that I still have a bald spot from the time you put hair remover on my scalp when I fell asleep during that personal hygiene film strip. And I hate wearing hats!

Sincerely,
Miss Shmortley

P.S. – I see you used "Dear" in your salutation. I suppose that could be considered "good," at least for you.

 EGAD! SHMORTLEY IS RIGHT!
I DID USE "DEAR"!

EGAD.? WHO SAYS THAT
ANYMORE.?

 I DO. WHICH MEANS IT'S COOL. YOU
CAN'T EXPECT ME TO SAY "ACK!"
EVERY TIME THINGS DON'T GO MY
WAY.

I SUPPOSE THAT WOULD
GET BORING, SINCE THINGS DON'T
GO YOUR WAY A LOT.

 ACK!

Regardless of whether or not I showed any traces of goodness when I was younger, I'm definitely showing traces *now*! Maybe it just took cloning myself to realize that I'm not the totally, thoroughly, absolutely evil mastermind I thought I was. Dad is going to be so disappointed, but I'm going to have to tell him sooner or later.

Sooner or later . . .

WELL, SON, JUST WHAT IS IT THAT'S SO BLASTED IMPORTANT THAT I HAD TO STOP WHACKING THE RETIREMENT HOME NURSES WITH MY CANE AND RUSH ON OVER HERE?

 I HAVE SOME TERRIBLE NEWS, DAD.

DON'T TELL ME—YOU ACCIDENTALLY SHRINK-RAYED ALL YOUR UNDERWEAR AGAIN.

 I'M AFRAID IT'S WORSE THAN THAT. I'M PRETTY SURE THAT I'M . . . NOT COMPLETELY EVIL.

WHAT?! OF COURSE YOU'RE EVIL! YOU COME FROM A LONG LINE OF DESPICABLE, DASTARDLY, DOWNRIGHT DIABOLICAL INCOMPREHENSIBLES. WHERE IN THE HECK DID YOU COME UP WITH THIS "NOT COMPLETELY EVIL" NONSENSE?

FOR ONE THING, I HELD THE DOOR OPEN FOR AN ELDERLY WOMAN AT THE GROCERY STORE TODAY. I'M SO ASHAMED. . . .

THAT, MY SINISTER SON, WAS *BRILLIANTLY* EVIL! I HAPPENED TO BE AT THE CHECKOUT PAYING FOR TEN POUNDS OF ASPARAGUS WITH A BAGFUL OF PENNIES AND SAW THE WHOLE THING. RARELY HAVE I BEEN SO PROUD!

WELL, I ALSO SENT MY SEVENTH-GRADE TEACHER AN E-MAIL THAT BEGAN WITH "DEAR MISS SHMORTLEY." *DEAR!* I AM NOT WORTHY TO BEAR THE NAME INCOMPREHENSIBLE.

OH, BALONEY. YOU WERE OBVIOUSLY TELLING HER SHE LOOKS LIKE A "DEER." I REMEMBER DROOGENVINIA, AND YOU'RE RIGHT ON THE MONEY WITH THAT ONE.

 MAYBE YOU'RE RIGHT. BUT HOW DO YOU EXPLAIN THE FACT THAT I HAVE NEVER TAKEN OVER THE WORLD? OR DISPOSED OF COMMANDER VIRTUE?

AH, SON—THAT'S NOT A SHORTAGE OF *EVIL.* THAT'S A SHORTAGE OF *ABILITY.* YOU'RE JUST NOT A VERY GOOD SUPERVILLAIN. THAT'S NOTHING TO BE ASHAMED OF. I NEVER RULED THE WORLD, EITHER.

BUT I HAVE TARNISHED THE FAMILY NAME.

NONSENSE.
NO INCOMPREHENSIBLE
HAS EVER RULED THE WORLD.
NOT EVEN FOR A MINUTE.

BUT I THOUGHT THE INCOMPREHENSIBLES HAVE BEEN MAKING LIFE MISERABLE FOR HUMANITY FOR CENTURIES. LOOK, I STILL CARRY AROUND THIS TORN PHOTO OF GRAMPA HERBERT THE INCOMPREHENSIBLE AND HE SURE LOOKS LIKE HE'S RULING SOMETHING.

AND I STILL CARRY AROUND THE
REST OF THAT PHOTO.
DON'T ASK ME WHY.

Me at the movies, Summer 1955
–Herbert the Incomprehensible

 OH.

LOOK, SON. THE BOTTOM LINE IS
THE INCOMPREHENSIBLES HAVEN'T
BEEN A VERY SUCCESSFUL LOT. BUT
THAT DOESN'T MEAN WE DON'T TRY.
AND IT SURE AS SHERBET DOESN'T
MEAN WE AREN'T *EVIL*.

HELLO, SIR. IT'S A PLEASURE TO MEET YOU. I MUST SAY, YOU'RE LOOKING RATHER DAPPER IN THAT HANDSOME EYE PATCH. WELL, I MUST BE RUNNING ALONG NOW. I'M GOING DOOR-TO-DOOR COLLECTING RECYCLABLE CANS FOR CHARITY. HAVE A NICE DAY.

NOW WHO IN SNORZOK'S NAME WAS THAT?

OH, HIM? THAT'S JUST MY CLONE.

HE'S YOUR CLONE?! ALL RIGHT, FORGET EVERYTHING I JUST SAID. YOU OBVIOUSLY ARE NOT EVIL. I BLAME YOUR MOTHER. I'M HEADING BACK TO THE RETIREMENT HOME AND I'D APPRECIATE IT IF YOU DIDN'T VISIT ME ANYMORE—NOT THAT YOU EVER DID. ACK! I'M NEVER GOING TO LIVE THIS DOWN!

This is bad, Armageddon. I haven't seen my father this disappointed since Captain America got his own comic book. It's going to be quite a challenge to regain my ultra evilness . . . and his respect. The way I see it, I have two choices. I can either meet this challenge head-on like a true Supervillain or roll up into a pathetic little ball of sorrow and shame.

 *OH, WHAT IS IT, ARMAGEDDON? CAN'T YOU SEE I'M ROLLED UP INTO A PATHETIC LITTLE BALL OF SORROW AND SHAME?*

BY THE FOUL-SMELLING FEET OF FLOOBAR, ARMAGEDDON! You're right! Vordak the Incomprehensible never runs away from a challenge—unless I know for sure that that challenge is slower than I am. *I WILL get back to my old evil self! I WILL transform Vordy into the Supervillain he was meant to be! And I WILL make myself a peanut butter and jelly sandwich! I'm starving!*

CHAPTER SEVEN

Ah, a good night's sleep can really help clear the mind, even one as clearly magnifulous as my own.

"Umm, magnifulous? That isn't even a word."

Of course it's a word! It just happens to be one I created myself. My mind happens to be both magnificent *and* fabulous, so it makes sense to combine the words in order to save time. You wouldn't understand.

"Sure I would. You're also quite shumpy."

Hmm, shrewd and grumpy—not bad. I have been a bit of a grouch lately.

"No, short and dumpy."

You know what? I'm not even going to unleash my fabled fury upon you for that comment. I'm not going to call you a dimwitted doofus or a ham-headed halfwit or even a great galloping goober. And I'm not going to say that I've seen bowling balls that were sharper than you. No, I'm not going to do any of that because I have more important things on my mind. I need to stay calm and under control as I carefully plot my next move. Nothing that you do or say can possibly make me lose my cool at this, the most critical moment in my villainous career.

"sure thing, shumpy."

THAT'S IT, YOU . . . YOU . . . YOU . . . *ACK!!* I used up all my best insults in that last paragraph! Nevertheless, your ridiculous rambling is giving me a headache. So I'm going to use my shrink ray to reduce your comments down to a size that is unreadable.

"wait a minute. That's not fair! you can't do that! ———

Ah, that's much better. I can finally think clearly without all that bird-brained blabbering going on. And with clear thoughts come brilliant ideas from Vordak the Incomprehensible! For example . . .

Freds!

FREDS!

FREDS!

YES, YOUR SOMEWHAT EVILNESS. WE WERE PLAYING FOOTBALL IN THE YARD AND GOT HERE AS QUICKLY AS WE COULD.

I NEED THE SEVEN OF YOU TO GET TO WORK IMMEDIATELY ON—

EIGHT.

EXCUSE ME?

YOU CAN'T REALLY MAKE FAIR TEAMS WITH SEVEN, SO THERE ARE EIGHT OF US NOW.

WELL, OF **COURSE** THERE ARE. HOW SILLY OF ME TO THINK I COULD GO MORE THAN A FEW HOURS WITHOUT FACING THE FURTHER INFLATION OF THE FABLED FRED FORCE. I NEED THE **EIGHT** OF YOU TO GET TO WORK IMMEDIATELY ON A DEVICE THAT WILL REMOVE ALL THE GOOD FROM A PERSON, LEAVING THEM 100 PERCENT EVIL FROM HEAD TO TOE.

AGAIN, WE'RE CLONING SCIENTISTS, NOT GOODNESS-REMOVAL SCIENTISTS.

THAT'S FUNNY, BECAUSE YOU'RE BEGINNING TO LOOK LIKE DISSOLVED-IN-BOILING-YOGURT SCIENTISTS TO ME!

COME TO THINK OF IT, WE **DO** REMEMBER READING A BOOK ABOUT GOODNESS REMOVAL A FEW YEARS BACK, SO SURE! WE CAN TAKE CARE OF THAT FOR YOU! WOULD YOU LIKE THE GOODNESS SUCKED OUT, BLOWN OUT, YANKED OUT, OR JUST SLOWLY DRAINED?

SUCKED OUT IS FINE. THEN I CAN CALL THE DEVICE MY VILLAINOUS VORCUUM! NOTHING GRABS ATTENTION LIKE A COOL-SOUNDING NAME.

WE WOULDN'T KNOW.

WELL? DON'T JUST STAND THERE—GET TO WORK! I NEED TO SUCK ALL THE **GOOD** OUT OF MY CLONE AS SOON AS POSSIBLE. HE'S REALLY BEGINNING TO EMBARRASS ME.

WE'LL HOP RIGHT ON IT, YOUR MODERATELY EVILNESS. BUT BEFORE YOU GO, WE'VE NOTICED YOU HAVE BEEN A LITTLE DOWN LATELY, SO FRED HERE HAS A RIDDLE TO CHEER YOU UP.

 WHAT KINDS OF PETS DO CLONES PREFER?

 I DON'T KNOW. PARAKEETS.

NOPE.

 SALAMANDERS!

SORRY.

 WELL, **WHAT** THEN?! I DON'T HAVE ALL DAY!

COPYCATS. GET IT? COPYCATS?

 OH, FOR THE LOVE OF . . .

knock knock

WHO COULD THAT BE AT THE DOOR?

 WELL, FOR YOUR SAKES IT HAD BETTER NOT BE ANOTHER FRED! NOW GET DOWN TO THE LABORATORY AND DON'T COME BACK UP WITHOUT MY VORCUUM!

knock knock

 OH, HOLD ON! I'M COMING!

WELL?! WHAT IS IT?!

HELLO, SIR. MY NAME IS LILA AND I'M COLLECTING RECYCLABLE CANS FOR CHARITY. DO YOU HAVE ANY YOU WOULD LIKE TO DONATE?

NO. MY CLONE . . . ERR . . . *SON* ALREADY TOOK THEM ALL.

THAT'S WHAT I FIGURED, BUT I THOUGHT I WOULD ASK ANYWAY. HE LOOKS A LOT LIKE YOU, YOU KNOW?

WAIT. YOU KNOW MY CLONE . . . ERR . . . *SON?*

SURE! HE STARTED THIS WHOLE RECYCLABLE CAN COLLECTION PROJECT AND GOT A BUNCH OF US NEIGHBORHOOD KIDS TO HELP OUT. HE'S SUCH A NICE, GIVING PERSON. AND KINDA CUTE, TOO. BUT DON'T TELL HIM I SAID THAT. YOU MUST BE VERY PROUD, SIR.

(SIGH) OH, YES . . . *VERY* PROUD. NOW TELL ME WHERE HE IS IMMEDIATELY! I HAVE BEEN LOOKING FOR HIM!

HE'S OUT BACK BY THE TREE HOUSE.

TREE HOUSE?

Since when is there a tree house in my yard, Armageddon? And, more importantly, why have I not been invited up to check it out? I *love* tree houses. I remember when I was young, my dad built me one in our sinister sycamore. It had everything: two stories, carpeting, barbed wire around the railings, steel drums filled with acid. It even had electricity. It was the most spectacular tree house in the entire city! At least that's what he told me. I never actually got to see the inside because Dad made the opening too small for my helmet to fit through. He ended up taking a TV up there and spent many a summer evening with his buddies watching baseball and playing cards. I could hear them while I sat all by myself in my room making little henchman figures out of paper clips and Play-Doh. . . . It always sounded like they were having so much fun up there. . . .

HEY, VORDAK!
I DIDN'T SEE YOU STANDING OVER
THERE. WAIT A MINUTE. . . .
ARE YOU *CRYING*?

(SNIFF) OF COURSE NOT! VORDAK
THE INCOMPREHENSIBLE DOES NOT
CRY! I'VE, UH . . . BEEN WORKING
OUT! THAT'S JUST FOREHEAD
SWEAT RUNNING DOWN MY CHEEK.
AND A GNAT FLEW INTO MY EYE!
AND ONE OF THE NEIGHBOR KIDS
SHOT ME WITH A SQUIRT GUN. AND
MY CONTACT LENS HAS A TEAR IN
IT! BUT THAT'S NOT IMPORTANT.
WHAT'S GOING ON OUT HERE?

WELL, LIKE I SAID WHEN OUR FATHER
WAS OVER, I WAS GOING DOOR-TO-DOOR
COLLECTING CANS TO TAKE TO THE
RECYCLING CENTER AND GIVE WHATEVER
MONEY I GOT TO CHARITY.

UGH. DON'T REMIND ME.

ANYWAY, I FIGURED MORE
PEOPLE COLLECTING CANS
WOULD MEAN EVEN MORE
MONEY FOR CHARITY, SO I WENT
AROUND THE NEIGHBORHOOD LOOKING
FOR KIDS TO HELP AND, WELL, HERE
WE ARE. LILA HERE EVEN CAME UP
WITH A NAME FOR US.

WE'RE THE SUPER SMILEY RAINBOW
PONY RECYCLING CLUB!

OH, GOOD GRIEF, VORDY! WE NEED
TO TALK. I REALIZE YOU AREN'T
COMPLETELY EVIL, BUT THIS IS JUST
PLAIN EMBARRASSING. YOU SIMPLY
CAN'T GO AROUND AND . . .
*WHAT IN KLORZAR'S NAME ARE YOU
WEARING?*

WE HAD T-SHIRTS MADE.
PRETTY NEAT, HUH?

 WHY ARE YOU DOING THIS TO ME, VORDY?! ALL I WANTED WAS SOMEONE TO FOLLOW IN MY EVIL FOOTSTEPS. SOMEONE WITH WHOM I COULD WIN THE GLORIOUS GAMES AND THEN CONQUER THE PLANET WITH, SIDE BY SIDE. SOMEONE THAT I COULD RULE THE WORLD WITH, HELPING ME TO HEARTLESSLY HEAVE HEAPS OF HARDSHIP ONTO THE HAPLESS HORDES OF HUMANITY. AND THIS IS WHAT I GET. HOW MUCH ARE THESE CANS EVEN WORTH?

OH, THAT'S DELBERT'S DEPARTMENT.

IT'S QUITE SIMPLE, REALLY. ONE EMPTY 12-OUNCE CAN WEIGHS APPROXIMATELY 14 GRAMS, WHICH EQUALS .4938 OUNCES. THERE ARE 16 OUNCES IN 1 POUND SO, BY DIVIDING 16 BY .4938, YOU GET 32.4 CANS PER POUND. THE LOCAL RECYCLING CENTER PAYS 65 CENTS PER POUND FOR ALUMINUM. SO, BY DIVIDING 1 DOLLAR BY 65 CENTS AND THEN MULTIPLYING THE RESULT BY 32.4, YOU CAN EASILY DETERMINE THAT WE WILL RECEIVE 1 DOLLAR FOR EVERY 50 CANS WE RECYCLE. APPROXIMATELY.

 *OH. SAY, YOU WOULDN'T HAPPEN TO BE EVIL, WOULD YOU, DELBERT?*

NO, SIR.

 THAT'S TOO BAD. I WAS JUST THINKING HOW I COULD USE A NEW SCIENTIST.

CHAPTER EIGHT

Vordak the Incomprehensible's clone . . . doing *charity work*! I'll be laughed out of the Supervillain Softball League! They'll remove my name from the Supervillain Directory! They'll cancel my membership to the Supervillain Swim Club!

Oh, for the love of lip lard, Armageddon, what is it?

So, you've got my vPad. What on earth do you want me to do with that? Check my e-mail? Play a game? Search for cat videos on YouTube? *What?*

You want me to *read* it? Well, hand it over, then. And there had better not be any slobber on it!

Janitor and Lunch Lady Retire from Local Junior High School

Farding Junior High School has lost two of its most beloved staff members, as longtime janitor Burfus Waxclog and lunch lady Agnes Lipwartz have unexpectedly decided to retire. They had been with the school for over fifteen years.

The pair cited the difficulty in performing their separate jobs ever since their bodies were fused together in an unfortunate matter-transporter accident as the reason for calling it quits. "It's nearly impossible," claimed Waxclog, "to unplug a sink in the locker room while at the same time serving sliced carrots in the cafeteria."

Lipwartz shared her half step-cousin's concerns. "There I would be with a serving fork in one hand and a pipe wrench in the other and I would keep dipping the wrench into the baked beans by mistake. It was all so confusing." The matter transporter, a science-fair project created by seventh grader Vordak the Incomprehensible, had received a "Participant" ribbon by the fair's judges.

The pair, who recently purchased a new home, was asked what they planned to do with themselves now that their days were free. "Gardening," replied Lipwartz. "Lots and lots of gardening. And building a powerful death ray, which we will use to destroy Vordak the Incomprehensible and his secret underground lair. And probably some scrapbooking."

Ahhhh, although your comments are too small for me to see, dear reader, I sense that you are confused about Waxclog and Lipwartz. Of course, you are always confused about something, so I may just be sensing *that*.

"Thfug njhhfifu nd ndjfdoajhf nohdf n ondikfi modud hngj hg a dlhdur ljdfnc!"

Oh, pipe down. I'll give you a quick recap. You know, if you'd have read *Rule the School*, I wouldn't have to waste my time filling you in. Anyway, about sixteen years ago, this happened:

Blast from evil ray buries apartment building in earthworms

Burfus Waxclog

Agnes Lipwartz

Vordak The Incomprehensible

Residents of the Shady Plains apartment complex were awakened late last night by the sight and sound and smell and taste of tens of millions of earthworms bombarding their building. No one was injured. Local Supervillain Vordak the Incomprehensible is believed to be responsible.

When asked about the ray blast, Incomprehensible claimed it was simply a big misunderstanding. "I was minding my own business, testing my Wondrously Wicked Worm Ray, and had it aimed at an empty field. Just as I began to pull the activation lever, I sneezed. And my arm got tangled in my cape. And the phone rang. Then, before you know it, the sun was in my eyes. I may have bumped the ray slightly off target without realizing it, but as you can see, it was due to circumstances that were completely beyond my control."

Two residents of the apartment building, Burfus Waxclog and his half step-cousin Agnes Lipwartz, lost everything they had in the slimy downpour. "You ever try to clean a sofa that's been buried in worm guts?" lamented Waxclog. "That stuff doesn't come out." When told that Incomprehensible insisted he had meant no harm with his Wondrously Wicked Worm Ray, Waxclog was irate. "Are you kidding me? He's got the word *Wicked* right there in the name, for cryin' out loud!" Lipwartz said she had been in contact with Incomprehensible and when she asked him what he had to say for himself, he simply responded, "MUAHAHAHAHA!!"

As I clearly stated in the article, that whole incident was not my fault. I mean, if you don't want to be buried in earthworms, then don't live near someone who has a Wondrously Wicked Worm Ray. And if anyone had the right to be upset, it was me. Lipwartz and Waxclog never even returned my worms! The nerve, right?

Well, after last year's accident with my Abominable Age-Reduction Ray, I found myself back in junior high . . . and guess who the janitor and lunch lady were? Exactly: Waxclog and Lipwartz. And they had it out for me from day one, I tell you! Even though I was nothing but a studious, well-behaved student.

They nosed around in the Miraculous Matter Transporter I innocently created for the science fair. And this happened:

Not my fault, right? If you ask me, they owe *me* an apology for messing around with my personal property! And now they want to use a death ray to destroy me and my secret underground lair? Ha! Let them try!

CHAPTER NINE

When it comes to transforming Vordy into a diabolical villain, I probably shouldn't put all my evil eggs in one basket. Based on what I've seen so far from the Freds, it would be a huge mistake to rely on them to successfully construct my Villainous Vorcuum. Sure, it *might* happen, just like the earth *might* stop orbiting the sun ... and bats *might* fly out of my nose ... and someone somewhere *might* think I am not inconceivably handsome. And since I'm just sitting around and waiting on the Freds anyway, I may as well take matters into my own hands and try to convert Vordy to evil the old-fashioned way.

ALL RIGHT, VORDY. I HAVE DECIDED THAT IT'S TIME FOR ME TO TAKE A MORE ACTIVE ROLE IN SOLVING YOUR LITTLE PROBLEM.

WHAT LITTLE PROBLEM?

THE FACT THAT YOU'RE NOT EVIL! GOOD GRAVY, VORDY, HAVEN'T YOU BEEN PAYING ATTENTION?

BUT I DON'T CONSIDER THAT TO BE A PROBLEM AT ALL. QUITE THE OPPOSITE, IN FACT. WHEN I DO SOMETHING GOOD, LIKE COLLECTING CANS OR HELPING MRS. TWARDZIK TAKE OUT HER TRASH, IT MAKES ME FEEL ALL WARM AND FUZZY INSIDE.

AND IT MAKES ME FEEL LIKE THROWING MY INSIDES UP! LOOK, I KNOW THAT YOUR HEART MUST STILL CONTAIN **SOME** EVIL, AT LEAST ONE VALVE OR SOMETHING. AND I ALSO KNOW THAT, GIVEN THE CHANCE, THAT EVIL PART WILL RISE TO THE SURFACE—IT WILL GROW AND SPREAD UNTIL YOUR ENTIRE HEART BEATS WITH INCOMPREHENSIBLE BADNESS! MUAHAHAHAHA!!!

WHY WOULD I WANT IT TO DO THAT?

BECAUSE IT'S WHO YOU ARE. AND I CAN PROVE IT.

I PUT TOGETHER A BOX OF THINGS THAT YOU CAN USE TO HELP GET YOUR EVIL JUICES FLOWING AGAIN. NOW, SEE THAT LARGE PICTURE WINDOW IN THE FRONT OF MRS. TWARDZIK'S HOUSE?

SURE.

AND SEE THAT VASE ON THE TABLE?

YUP. IT'S LOVELY.

LOVELY? SERIOUSLY? VORDY, YOU ARE KILLING ME HERE. LOOK, SHE KEEPS HER FAVORITE THING SHE OWNS ON THAT TABLE IN THE WINDOW. IT USED TO BE A UNICORN FIGURINE, THEN IT WAS A PICTURE OF SOME ACTOR SHE MET ONCE, AND NOW IT'S THAT RIDICULOUS VASE. AND SHE CLEANS THE WINDOW THREE TIMES A DAY SO THE WHOLE NEIGHBORHOOD CAN GET A GOOD LOOK AT HER PRIZED POSSESSION. NOW, HERE—TAKE THESE.

ROCKS? WHAT SHOULD I DO WITH THESE?

ISN'T IT OBVIOUS? MRS. TWARDZIK CHERISHES HER WINDOW DISPLAY. SHE PAINSTAKINGLY CLEANS THAT WINDOW THREE TIMES A DAY. YOU HAVE A HANDFUL OF ROCKS. THINK ABOUT IT.

OH, I GET IT. BUT ARE YOU SURE THIS IS SOMETHING I OUGHT TO BE DOING?

IF YOU'RE AN INCOMPREHENSIBLE, IT IS. AND YOU ARE. SO IT IS. NOW GET GOING!

And so my young clone's reign of non-terror is about to come to an end! Once he feels the thrill of evildoing, he will be transformed into the unscrupulous scoundrel I was at his age. Am I brilliant or what?

Did you hear me, reader? I said, "Am I brilliant or what?"

"R Fhty hhf tyghju wee I rkejfdu mnjdhery uumd rt iaedjn."

Ah, that's right. I shrunk all your comments. You know what? I'm in such a good mood, what with Vordy about to turn evil and all, that I am going to give you a second chance. I recommend you don't blow it.

"what the heck?! you are such a jerk that *ikejfdu mnjdhery uumd rt iaedjn..."*

Aaaaand you blew it. It's back to shrunken comments for you.

∎ ▪ ▪ ▪ ▪ ▪ ▪ ▪ ▪ ▪ ▪ ▪

I wonder what's taking Vordy so long. And why haven't I heard the crash of . . . *Ah*, here he comes now. And he has a huge grin on his face! It worked! He loves being evil!

WELL, HOW DID IT GO?

FANTASTIC! MRS. TWARDZIK WAS SO SURPRISED SHE NEARLY PASSED OUT. YOU WERE RIGHT— THIS *DOES* FEEL GREAT!

OF COURSE I WAS RIGHT. I AM VORDAK THE INCOMPREHENSIBLE! LET ME JUST GRAB MY BINOCULARS AND TAKE A GOOD LOOK AT THE DAMAGE.

 GREAT GASSY GOBLINS! WHAT HAVE YOU DONE?!

PRETTY SWEET ROCK TURTLE, EH? LIKE I SAID, MRS. TWARDZIK WAS TOTALLY SURPRISED. SHE SAID SHE LOVED IT SO MUCH THAT SHE WAS GOING TO PUT IT ON THE DISPLAY TABLE.

 YOU DIDN'T THROW **ANY** OF THE ROCKS AT THE WINDOW?

OF COURSE NOT. THAT WOULD HAVE BROKEN IT.

 **ACK! THAT'S THE POINT!** ALL RIGHT, PERHAPS YOU WEREN'T READY FOR SOMETHING **THAT** EVIL RIGHT OFF THE BAT. LET'S SEE WHAT ELSE IS IN THE BOX. AH, HERE WE GO.

THANKS, BUT I DON'T HAVE TO
GO RIGHT NOW.

IT'S NOT FOR YOU, YOU MADDENING
MINI ME! IT'S FOR MRS. TWARDZIK.
YOU'RE GOING TO TOILET-PAPER HER
HOUSE. NOW, DO YOU THINK YOU CAN
HANDLE THAT?

SURE, I GUESS SO. YOU'RE RIGHT—THAT
ISN'T NEARLY AS BAD AS THROWING
ROCKS THROUGH HER WINDOW.
I JUST HOPE SHE DOESN'T MIND.

OF COURSE SHE'S GOING TO MIND!
THAT'S THE WHOLE POINT!
NOW GET MOVING!

Ah, how I miss toilet-papering homes. The awesome sight of a well-thrown roll arcing gracefully over a tree or shrub. The look of surprise and horror as the home's occupant steps outside and witnesses the carnage. Such a simple yet vastly rewarding exercise in evil!

Here comes Vordy now, grinning ear to ear with satisfaction. And this time it is obviously due to the villainy he has dealt out.

 NOW, THAT FELT GOOD, DIDN'T IT?

ABSOLUTELY! I WAS IN AND OUT SO FAST SHE HARDLY KNEW WHAT HIT HER! MAN, THAT WAS A RUSH!

 *EXCELLENT! I KNEW YOU HAD IT IN YOU. LET'S TAKE A LOOK AT THE DAMAGE!*

UH, WHERE'S THE TOILET PAPER?

ON THE DISPENSER IN HER BATHROOM, WHERE ELSE?

HER OLD ROLL WAS ALMOST EMPTY, TOO, SO THIS WAS PERFECT TIMING. BY THE WAY, SHE WANTS TO KNOW IF WE HAVE ANY PAPER TOWELS.

WHO **ARE** YOU?!

I'M YOU.

DON'T REMIND ME. YOU KNOW WHAT? I HAVE ONE MORE THING IN THIS BOX. TAKE IT.

 *IT'S A WATER BALLOON. MRS. TWARDZIK WALKS HER PATHETIC LITTLE POOCH EVERY DAY AT THIS TIME. SHE'LL BE OUT ON THE SIDEWALK, TOTALLY UNPROTECTED AND VULNERABLE. IN FACT, HERE SHE COMES NOW. GO DO YOUR THING!*

This should be interesting. I don't know how he could possibly screw *this* up, but I have no doubt he'll find a way.

Aaaaaand there you go. It looks like it's the Vorcuum or nothing. Those Freds had best not disappoint me. I need a nap.

CHAPTER TEN

HERE YOU ARE, YOUR NOT QUITE COMPLETELY EVILNESS. ONE STATE-OF-THE-ART, CUTTING-EDGE, HIGHLY ADVANCED VORCUUM, AS REQUESTED.

HMMM, IT CERTAINLY DOESN'T LOOK VERY IMPRESSIVE.

WE MADE IT OUT OF AN OLD VACUUM CLEANER TO SAVE TIME. BUT LOOK—WE WROTE VORCUUM ON IT!

WELL, HOW DOES IT WORK?

SIMPLE. JUST PLACE THE MASK OVER THE FACE, SET THE LEVER TO **SUCK**, AND TURN IT ON. THE VORCUUM WILL SHUT OFF AUTOMATICALLY WHEN ALL THE GOOD HAS BEEN SUCKED OUT. THERE IS A GAUGE ON THE TOP THAT INDICATES WHEN THE TANK IS FULL.

GOODNESS GAUGE

E F

Vorcuum

HOW DO YOU EVEN KNOW IF THIS THING WILL ACTUALLY WORK?

ON A PERSON? UHH . . .
TO BE HONEST, WE DON'T.

WELL, WHY IN TRAZNOR'S
NAME DIDN'T YOU TEST IT ON ONE OF
YOURSELVES? THAT'S WHAT YOU'RE
THERE FOR!

THE MASK WON'T SEAL PROPERLY
ON ONE OF US. YOU **HAVE** SEEN OUR
NOSES, RIGHT?

WELL THEN, WE'LL JUST HAVE TO
TEST IT ON SOMEONE ELSE. AND I
KNOW JUST THE SOMEONE.

OH, DELBERT!
COULD YOU COME HERE
FOR A MOMENT?

DELBERT, YOU SEEM LIKE A BRIGHT YOUNG MAN. HOW WOULD YOU LIKE TO BE INVOLVED IN AN . . . . EXPERIMENT?

WOULD I? I *LOVE* EXPERIMENTS! WHY, JUST THE OTHER DAY I WAS COMBINING SODIUM CHLORMANTHILTRATE WITH POTASSIUM SULMIFATE AND—

 I'M IN A HURRY, DELBERT, SO LET'S JUST GET ON WITH IT, SHALL WE?

WAIT. WHAT IS YOUR HYPOTHESIS?

 MY WHAT?

ACCORDING TO THE SCIENTIFIC METHOD, AN EXPERIMENT IS CONDUCTED TO PROVE OR DISPROVE A HYPOTHESIS. SO WHAT'S YOURS?

 MY HYPOTHESIS IS THAT YOU ARE WEARING MY PATIENCE TO THE BONE, YOU BESPECTACLED BARNACLE BRAIN!

THAT'S REALLY MORE OF A STATEMENT THAN A HYPOTHESIS.

AND YOU'RE REALLY MORE OF A PAIN IN MY BACKSIDE THAN I CAN BEAR! NOW STAND STILL SO WE CAN PROCEED WITH THE EXPERIMENT.

OKAY. BUT TECHNICALLY, WITHOUT A HYPOTHESIS, THIS ISN'T REALLY AN EXPERIMENT. IT'S JUST A THING THAT YOU'RE DOING.

ACK! FREDS, PROCEED WITH THE EXPERI . . . *THING THAT WE'RE DOING!* AT LEAST THE MASK WILL MUFFLE THE SOUND OF HIS VOICE!

IT WORKED! IT ACTUALLY WORKED! THERE DOESN'T APPEAR TO BE SO MUCH AS A GRAIN-SIZE GLIMMER OF GOODNESS REMAINING IN HIM! TELL ME, DELBERT—HOW DO YOU FEEL?

THAT'S DOCTOR DIABOLICAL TO YOU, YOU FLATULENT FATHEAD! HOW DO I FEEL? A LOT BETTER THAN YOU WILL AFTER THIS—

ACK! I HAVE A FEELING THIS MAY COME BACK TO HAUNT ME— PARTICULARLY IF I WRITE ANOTHER BOOK.

SO WE TAKE IT YOU'RE PLEASED? ASIDE FROM THE SHIN KICK, THAT IS?

 OF COURSE I'M PLEASED! WHY WOULDN'T I BE? MY VILLAINOUS VORCUUM IS A COMPLETE AND UTTER SUCCESS, AND I HAVE ONCE AGAIN PROVEN MYSELF TO BE BRILLIANT BEYOND COMPARE!

EXCUSE US, YOUR FAIRLY EVILNESS, BUT WE—

 *BUT YOU WHAT? LOOK FORWARD TO YOUR BATH IN BOILING YOGURT?*

The nerve of some toadies. Expecting credit for something that I clearly accomplished almost entirely on my own! Whose idea was it in the first place? MINE! So they developed the technology and designed and assembled all the parts. Big deal. Who named it the Vorcuum? *ME*, that's who!

AND NOW TO USE THE VILLAINOUS VORCUUM ON VORDY!

YOU'LL HAVE TO EMPTY IT FIRST. ACCORDING TO THE GAUGE, IT'S FULL. THAT DELBERT SURE WAS ONE SWEET KID.

BAH! THEN I DID THE WORLD A FAVOR. HOW DO I DISPOSE OF ALL THAT GOODNESS?

JUST SET THE LEVER TO *BLOW* AND TURN IT ON.

GREAT GOOEY GLOBS OF GOODNESS! *That* was disgusting. Armageddon, find Vordy and bring him here immediately. I cannot bear the thought of my cloned copy overflowing with these particles of appalling pleasantness. And once Vordy is re-evilized, I'll use the Vorcuum on myself. The mere thought of those nasty niblets of niceness nestled near my nervous system is enough to make me nearly nauseous.

While I await my clone's arrival, I have decided to grace you, undeserving reader, with a priceless piece of positively preeminent poetry. Your comments are, thankfully, still too tiny to read, so I will just assume you are grateful beyond measure. I call this piece "Evilosity," and I'm making it up as I go.

EVILOSITY

In all your bookly reading,
I know you'll never see
Another rogue with my amount
Of Evilosity.

Not Voldemort or Olaf,
Not Wicked Witch of West.
When it comes to Evilosity
I, Vordak, am the best!

That Grinch can be a mean one
At least until Whos sing
But I am awful all the time
That's just my evil thing.

Captain Hook is quite the villain
Just go ask Peter Pan
But I am far more evil
And I still have my left hand.

So put those other tomes aside
My books are all you'll need
To learn of Evilosity
. . . Assuming you can read.

My—that was a *magnificent* effort, even for me! Verily, it doth well nigh bring a tear to mine eye! (That was fancy literary language meant to impress you—don't feel bad if you aren't bright enough to understand it.)

Ah, here comes Vordy now!

BY THE FLATTENED FEET OF FRAMNOR! WHAT DO MINE TROUBLED EYES REVEAL? VERILY?

I JUST THOUGHT I MIGHT WANT TO GIVE BEING A SUPERHERO A TRY. AND, BY THE WAY, YOUR FANCY LITERARY LANGUAGE DOESN'T IMPRESS ME.

**ACK!
A SUPER . . . _HERO_?!
BUT WHY?!**

IT JUST SEEMS TO FIT THIS
WHOLE "GOOD" THING I'VE GOT GOING
ON BETTER THAN BEING A VILLAIN.
WHAT'S THAT YOU'VE GOT THERE?

**THIS IS MY VILLAINOUS VORCUUM!
IT SUCKS ALL THE GOODNESS OUT
OF A PERSON, LEAVING ONLY PURE
EVIL BEHIND! COME ON—LET'S HOOK
YOU UP.**

NAHHH, I DON'T THINK SO. THAT
WOULD PUT A REAL CRIMP IN THE
WHOLE SUPERHERO THING. I NEED TO
GO NOW. I'VE BEEN WORKING ON MY
CATCHPHRASE: **_LET JUSTICE PREVAIL!_**
WHAT DO YOU THINK?

**WAIT! DID I SAY IT SUCKS ALL THE
GOODNESS OUT OF A PERSON, LEAVING
ONLY PURE EVIL BEHIND? HOW SILLY
OF ME. WHAT I _MEANT_ TO SAY WAS
THAT IT CLEANS OUT YOUR AIR
PASSAGES SO YOU CAN MORE CLEARLY
SHOUT WARNINGS AND HEROIC
CATCHPHRASES AND SUCH.**

HEY, THAT WOULD BE **_PERFECT_** FOR ME!
CAN I TRY IT?

For crying out loud—I don't know if I should feel satisfaction that my trickery worked or embarrassment that I used to be this dimwitted. I guess I'll go with satisfaction. It won't matter in a few moments, anyway, when my true clone self is back and bristling with badness.

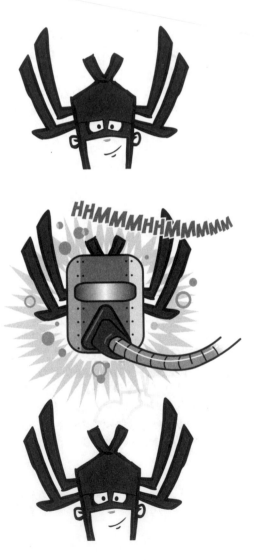

WHAT'S GOING ON? WHY DO YOU STILL HAVE THAT STUPID SMILE ON YOUR FACE?!

I DON'T KNOW. I'M JUST HAPPY, I GUESS. LET'S SEE IF IT WORKED.

LET JUSTICE PREVAIL!

HEY, THANKS. THAT'S *MUCH* BETTER. GOTTA GO.

FREDS! THE GAUGE! IT STILL READS **EMPTY!** NOT ONE MICRO-PARTICLE OF GOOD WAS SUCKED OUT OF MY CLONE! YOUR VORCUUM IS A FAILURE!

WE DON'T UNDERSTAND. EVERYTHING SEEMS TO BE IN WORKING ORDER. THERE IS SIMPLY NO GOOD EXPLANATION FOR THIS.

 OH, THERE'S A GOOD EXPLANATION, ALL RIGHT. YOU DON'T HAVE ONE WORKING BRAIN CELL BETWEEN THE EIGHT OF YOU AND—

NINE.

 . . . BETWEEN THE NINE OF YOU AND . . . **NINE?** WHEN DID YOU . . . **ACK!** NEVER MIND! IT NO LONGER MATTERS HOW MANY OF YOU THERE ARE. YOUR CONFOUNDED CONTRAPTION WORKED A WHOPPING **ONE** TIME! I CAN NO LONGER ENDURE THE INCOMPETENCE OF YOU INSUFFERABLE IMBECILES! IT'S THE VAT OF BOILING YOGURT FOR THE LOT OF YOU!

INCLUDING ME?

 OF COURSE INCLUDING YOU!

WHAT ABOUT ME?

YES, YOU, TOO! ACK! WHAT DO YOU THINK "THE LOT OF YOU" MEANS?

ALL RIGHT, JUST TO BE CLEAR ON THIS—ME, TOO?

ENOUGH! I WANT **ALL** OF YOU FEEBLE-MINDED FREDS—AND THAT INCLUDES YOU, YOU, **AND** YOU— TO REPORT TO MY BOILING-YOGURT TANK IN FIVE MINUTES.

WAIT A SECOND. IS THAT THE SAME THING AS YOUR YOGURT **VAT**? BECAUSE YOU'VE BEEN CALLING IT YOUR YOGURT **VAT** UP UNTIL NOW.

OF COURSE IT'S THE SAME THING! WHY WOULD I HAVE **TWO** ENORMOUS CONTAINERS OF YOGURT?!

YOU REALLY LIKE SMOOTHIES?

SLAM!

YOU'RE IN YOUR UNDERWEAR.

YUP. WELL, EXCEPT FOR
FRED BACK THERE. HE'S A BIT SHY.
THERE'S NO SENSE RUINING PERFECTLY
GOOD LAB COATS, TROUSERS, AND
SHOES, YOU KNOW?

**I SUPPOSE YOU'RE RIGHT. WELL,
CONGRATULATIONS—YOU HAVE NOW
UPPED THE NUMBER OF INTELLIGENT
THINGS YOU HAVE DONE SINCE
ARRIVING TO *ONE*!**

WE ALSO ALL PITCHED IN AND
GOT YOU THIS GIFT.

A GIFT? FOR ME? REALLY?

WHY . . . I DON'T KNOW WHAT TO SAY. OH, HOLD ON—YES I DO. *GET UP THAT LADDER!* KEEP YOUR SPACING, NOW! DON'T BUNCH UP! LET ONE FRED DISSOLVE COMPLETELY IN THE YOGURT BEFORE THE NEXT ONE JUMPS IN! I DON'T WANT ANY ACCIDENTS HERE!

Hmmm . . . now that's odd. I don't hear any screaming and crying and pleading for mercy. By the rotund rump of Ragnorak, I should be hearing screaming and crying and pleading for mercy! Something is amiss!

ACK! The boiling yogurt is not boiling! In fact, it's quite comfortable! That accursed sliver of goodness must have made me change the setting without realizing it!

THAT'S IT! EVERYBODY OUT!

OH, C'MON. CAN'T WE HAVE A FEW MORE MINUTES? WE WERE JUST SETTING UP A GAME OF SHARKS AND MINNOWS.

 *OUT!* EVERYBODY—JUST GET OUT, GET DOWN, AND GET OUT OF MY SIGHT! *FOREVER!* I DON'T WANT TO SO MUCH AS *SNIFF* ONE OF YOU BALLOON-NOSED BLOCKHEADS *EVER AGAIN!* DO YOU UNDERSTAND?!

EXCUSE ME, BUT WHEN YOU SAY "EVERYBODY," DOES THAT INCLUDE ME?

 ACK! AND DON'T FORGET TO TAKE THOSE IDIOTIC LAB COATS WITH YOU!

GREAT IDEA, FRED, TURNING THE VAT OFF BEFORE WE GAVE HIM THE VORCUUM.

CHAPTER ELEVEN

I must say, Armageddon, it feels great to finally be rid of those confounding Freds. My only regret is that I waited far too long to step up and stifle their startlingly stupendous stupitude. The way they kept multiplying, we're lucky there were only nine of them. At least I think there were only nine of them. I had better check the clone counter to make sure there aren't any extra copies lurking around that I don't know about.

All right now, they arrived as a duo, so that would mean seven more Freds were cloned. But one was copied because he stood too close to the leaky chamber when we made my 112-year-old clone, so that's really only six. Adding in my bone clone and Vordy makes 8, so they are all accounted for. Good!

Ah, yes—*good*. There is that word again. That awful, dreadful, sickening word. Whatever disgusting amount of good I have rattling around inside has ruined me as an evil Supervillain. It caused me to produce a clone that collects cans for charity and wants to be a Superhero. It made my dad ashamed of me. It won't even let me dispose of anyone in my diabolically clever death traps anymore.

And now . . . Armageddon, go and fetch Vordy, again. You both should hear this.

 SO, I SEE YOU'VE CHANGED BACK INTO YOUR SUPERVILLAIN GARB.

JUST UNTIL THE DRY CLEANER FINISHES POLISHING THE TRIM ON MY SUPERHERO COSTUME.

AH, BUT OF COURSE.

Anyway, I wanted to let you both know that I am going to be leaving you for a while. A long, long while. My good self has decided to turn my bad self in for all the evil I've done over the years. My bad self isn't very happy about this. In fact, my bad self wishes it could grab my good self by the neck and throw it down the Bottomless Pit of Plorzaz. But it can't, because my good self doesn't *have* a neck. It just sort of hangs around inside me and makes things miserable for my bad self.

So don't attempt to talk me out of it.

It would be pointless to even try.

Seriously, guys—my mind is made up.

OH, COME ON, NOW! Nothing? Really? Armageddon? After all these years? After all those walks?

Okay, then. I guess that's it. All that's left is to text Commander Virtue and offer my surrender.

U win I giv up

Excellent! Who is this?

Wat do u mean who is this? its your archnemesis! Your #1 enemy. The thorn in yor superheroic siide

Of course – Darkestro!

No not Darkestro! Who in zraflots name is darkstro? This is Vordk the incommptehensibl

Oh. Vordak. Well, your spelling is certainly incomprehensible. lol

I m texting witg my glovs on ha ha

Well, to each his own, I suppose. What is it you want? Are you issuing another ultimatum?

Actually . . . . . I m surrendrig

You're what?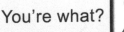

Surndering!

Surndering?

IM GIVNG UP U SQUARE JAWD SIMPLETN! IM TURNING MYSEF IN!

Ah, surrendering.
What brought this about, if I might ask?

it trns out i m only partly evil. and my good part has decided to giv up and reciev whatever punishmnt I have comming to me for all the harm my evil scheming has inflicted upon humanty.

I don't think humanity is even aware of your evil scheming. I always thwarted you before you really got going. Remember those escalators at the Crater Valley Mall?

I cant believe u brought that up again! really? the only reasn u defeated me was that the sun wwas in my eys. and they had just waxd the flors. and my cape got cought in the esclator when it started up again. otherwise it was a foolproof plan.

Sure. Anyway, I do appreciate your surrendering like this. Send me the address to your secret lair, and I will be by within the hour to pick you up – IN THE NAME OF TRUTH AND JUSTICE!

And 2 think we almost made it thru an entir convershation without u saying that . . .

Well, I guess that does it. A diabolically brilliant career in evil Supervillainy is about to come to an end. And to think the disgusting do-gooder who finally did me in was . . . me. Not Commander Virtue. Not Superman. Not Papa Smurf. Me.

Vordy, you're going to have to take care of Armageddon, what with me being imprisoned and all. He'll need to be walked, scratched behind the ears, and given a bath every three weeks or so. Oh, and you'll want to sneak up behind him at least seven times a day, yank his tail, and scream, *"Some watchdog you are!"* He loves that.

—Grrrrr

I keep his food down in the laboratory. Come along and I'll show you. But we need to hurry—that boasting barrel-chested blockhead, Commander Virtue, will be here any minute.

CHAPTER TWELVE

I keep Armageddon's food here, along with a few chew toys. He gets one cup in the morning and two cups at dinner and . . . *Hey, Armageddon*! What did I tell you about my statues? Go outside if you need to go to the bathroom.

RUFF!

WHAT?

RUFF!

 HUH?

RUFF!

 LOOK, I TOLD YOU—I DON'T UNDERSTAND DOG. YOU'RE JUST GOING TO HAVE TO DRAW ME ANOTHER PICTURE.

 YOU WANT ME TO COME OVER TO THE STATUE?

RUFF!

 WHAT?

Quite the smart aleck, are we now, Armageddon? I am well aware of the awesome beauty of this marble masterpiece. I come down here to gaze at it at least six times a day. I feel it accurately reflects my handsomeness and nobility and . . . Armageddon, what are you doing? Stop pulling on the arm or you're going to—

GREAT GASSY GOBLINS! It's a secret passageway! Oddly enough, it's a secret even to me! And, since I didn't put it there, it means that the person who *did* put it there can only be . . . *someone besides me!* Do you see, Vordy, how I have already used my brilliant mind to reduce the list of possible culprits by one? In order to narrow it down further, we will need to see where this passageway leads. Follow me.

Hmm, it is a bit dark in there. On second thought, *I'll* follow *you*. That way I will be able to protect the all-important rear flank.

 AHA! MY BRILLIANTLY VILLAINOUS MIND TELLS ME THIS IS A STORAGE CHAMBER OF SOME KIND. LET'S JUST TAKE A LITTLE PEEK INSIDE.

WAIT, WE CAN'T. IT SAYS *KEEP OUT* RIGHT THERE ON THE DOOR.

 ACK! YOU'RE RIGHT. WELL, THIS IS UNFORTUNATE. I SUPPOSE WE SHOULD KEEP MOVING ALONG AND . . . *HOLD ON A MINUTE!* THIS IS *MY EVIL LAIR* AND *I* WILL LOOK WHEREVER I PLEASE!

BUT IT SAYS *OR ELSE.*

THAT'S A GOOD POINT. **OR ELSE** DOES SOUND PRETTY BAD. WE'D BEST BE ON OUR WAY.

MY BRILLIANTLY VILLAINOUS MIND ALSO TELLS ME THAT WHOEVER BUILT THIS SECRET PASSAGEWAY HAS PLANS TO GET RID OF ME! WE'D BETTER KEEP MOVING.

GREAT GASSY GOBLINS!
VORDY, WE'RE IN YOUR TREE HOUSE!

AND THAT CAN ONLY MEAN ONE THING!

WELL, CONGRATULATIONS. YOU FINALLY—

THE BLUE BUZZARD IS TRYING TO DESTROY ME AND TAKE OVER THE WORLD!

HUH?

AND HE IS USING YOUR TREE HOUSE AS HIS COMMAND CENTER. HIS EVIL LAIR! IT'S ALL SO OBVIOUS NOW. *OF COURSE* THE BLUE BUZZARD WOULD CHOOSE A TREE-BASED LAIR! *OF COURSE* HE WANTS TO GET RID OF ME—HE KNOWS MY OWN AMBITIONS OF WORLD DOMINATION PRESENT THE GREATEST THREAT TO *HIS* TAKING OVER THE PLANET! AND LOOK HERE!

STORAGE CHAMBER 19b
SECURITY CAMERA

OF COURSE HE CREATED THE SECRET PASSAGEWAY TO GAIN ACCESS TO MY LABORATORY AND CREATE AN ARMY OF INDESTRUCTIBLE VORDY ROBOTS TO . . . ACTUALLY, THAT PART DOESN'T MAKE SO MUCH SENSE. WHY WOULDN'T HE HAVE MADE THEM LOOK LIKE HIMSELF? OR BUZZ?

BECAUSE IT'S NOT THE BLUE BUZZARD
YOU NEED TO WORRY ABOUT.

WHO, THEN? THE GREEN
GREMLIN?

NO.

THE PURPLE PLATYPUS?

NO!

THE BEIGE BULLFROG?

NO, YOU HAPLESS HAS-
BEEN! IT'S ME—VORDAK THE
INCOMPREHENSIBLE!

HOW DARE YOU USE ALLITERATION
ON ME! AND WHAT IN BLARVOTH'S
NAME ARE YOU TALKING ABOUT? WHY
WOULD I . . . ERR . . . YOU WANT TO
GET RID OF YOU . . . ERR . . . ME?
WE'RE THE SAME PERSON!

BECAUSE, LIKE I TOLD YOU
BACK WHEN YOU FIRST
CLONED ME—I DON'T LIKE BEING
CALLED VORDY! BUT DID YOU LISTEN?
NOOOOOO.

REALLY? THAT'S IT? OH, COME ON, NOW. WHEN I WAS YOUR AGE MY GRANDMOTHER, MILDRED THE INCOMPREHENSIBLE, USED TO CALL ME THAT WHENEVER SHE WANTED ME TO RUB HER FEET AND IT NEVER BOTHERED **ME**.

HA! I **AM** YOU AT MY AGE, REMEMBER? AND IT BOTHERS **ME**!

 ALL RIGHT, LOOK—I DIDN'T KNOW IT MEANT THAT MUCH TO YOU. I'LL CALL YOU VORDAK FROM NOW ON. BUT STILL, HOW COULD YOU POSSIBLY HAVE IT IN YOU TO GET RID OF ME? AFTER ALL, YOU'RE GOOD AND KIND AND DECENT AND ALL THAT RUBBISH.

YOU SALMON-BRAINED SIMPLETON! I DON'T HAVE ANY GOODNESS IN ME! I WAS FAKING IT. IT WAS ALL A CLEVER RUSE TO GET YOU TO DOUBT YOUR OWN EVILNESS. AND IT WORKED! MUAHAHAHAHA!!!

 BUT WHAT ABOUT ALL THOSE RECYCLABLE CANS YOU COLLECTED FOR CHARITY?

CHARITY, SHMARITY. WHAT DO YOU THINK I USED TO CREATE MY INDESTRUCTIBLE ROBOT ARMY!

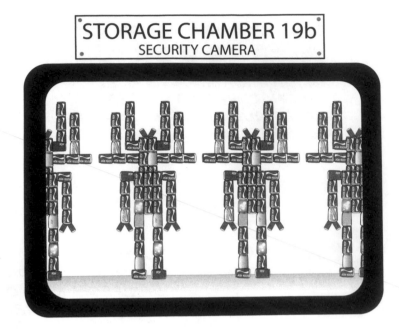

WELL, AT LEAST THIS EXPLAINS WHY THE VORCUUM DIDN'T APPEAR TO HAVE ANY EFFECT ON YOU. *WAIT A MINUTE!* IF YOU WERE FAKING IT, THAT MEANS *I* DON'T HAVE ANY GOODNESS IN *ME*, EITHER! *YES!* DAD IS GOING TO BE SO HAPPY.

IT'S TOO LATE FOR THAT. COMMANDER VIRTUE IS ON HIS WAY AS WE SPEAK, REMEMBER?

ACK! I FORGOT ABOUT THAT! BUT TOGETHER WE CAN FINALLY DEFEAT HIM—AND CONQUER THE PLANET!

SORRY, MY SAD-SACK SENIOR SELF, BUT I DECIDED I'M BETTER OFF WITHOUT YOU. WHEN YOU BRAGGED THAT WINNING THAT GLORIOUS GAMES TROPHY WOULD BE YOUR GREATEST ACCOMPLISHMENT, I KNEW I HAD TO GET RID OF YOU IF I HAD ANY HOPE OF RULING THE WORLD. FACE IT: AS A DIABOLICAL EVIL MENACE, YOU'VE BEEN A COMPLETE FAILURE. SAY, ARE THOSE COMMANDER VIRTUE'S PROPULSION BOOTS I HEAR?

GREAT GASSY GOBLINS, ARMAGEDDON! WE MUST HIDE!

AN UPSTANDING CITIZEN
IN A TREE HOUSE AROUND BACK
SAID I MIGHT FIND YOU HERE.

ACK! LOOK, I KNOW I SAID I WAS
GIVING MYSELF UP, BUT THAT WAS
BACK WHEN I THOUGHT I HAD SOME
GOOD IN ME. IT TURNS OUT I'M
COMPLETELY EVIL AFTER ALL, SO LET'S
JUST FORGET THE WHOLE THING AND
LET ME GO. WHAT DO
YOU SAY?

SORRY, VILE VILLAIN, BUT I'M AFRAID I
CAN'T DO THAT. *IN THE NAME OF TRUTH
AND JUSTICE,* YOU'RE COMING WITH ME!

I JUST REMEMBERED—I LEFT MY SPARE CAPE DOWN IN MY SECRET LABORATORY. DO YOU MIND IF WE GRAB IT BEFORE WE GO? THAT PRISON CELL MIGHT BE A BIT CHILLY.

I SUPPOSE THAT WOULD BE ALL RIGHT. JUST DON'T TRY ANY FUNNY BUSINESS.

HEY! WHAT'S GOING ON IN THERE?! YOU HAD BETTER NOT BE TRYING TO ESCAPE, SCOUNDREL!

SECRET LABORATORY

 *OH, DON'T GET YOUR TIGHTS IN A BUNCH, COMMANDER WORRYWART. I WAS JUST SHUTTING DOWN THE POWER TO MY LAB EQUIPMENT. SAY, DO YOU THINK THEY'LL PUT ME IN ONE OF THOSE COOL CUSTOM-BUILT PRISON CELLS? YOU KNOW, THE ONES WHERE THE WALLS AND FLOOR AND CEILING AND FURNITURE AND **EVERYTHING** IS MADE OF INDESTRUCTIBLE PLEXIGLAS INSTEAD OF METAL? LIKE THE ONE THEY USED FOR MAGNETO IN **X-MEN**?*

THAT DEPENDS. DO YOU POSSESS NEARLY UNIMAGINABLE MAGNETIC POWERS THAT ALLOW YOU TO MANIPULATE METAL IN ANY NUMBER OF DEADLY WAYS?

NO.

THEN I'M THINKING NO.

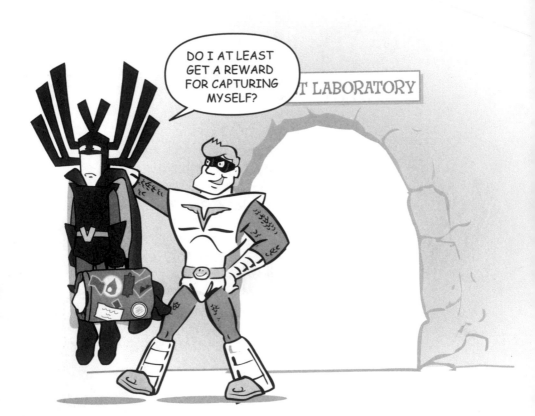

DO I AT LEAST GET A REWARD FOR CAPTURING MYSELF?

T LABORATORY

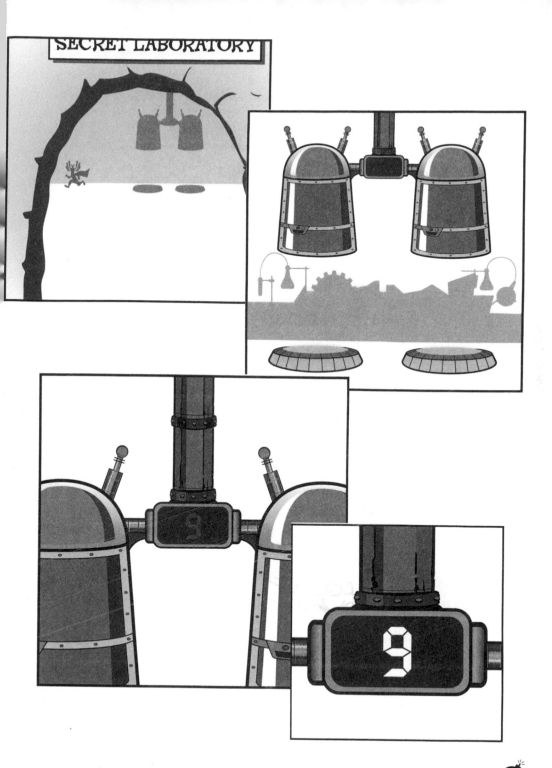

CHAPTER THIRTEEN

Now that I have finally rid myself of that older, lamer Vordak the Incomprehensible, it's only right that I take over his book. And trust me, you will be thankful I did. As you can see, I have already improved it by using a much fancier chapter heading. And a much nicer lettering style. And very expensive gray paper. I feel I'm worth it. Besides, you certainly don't want to follow the other Vordak's adventures in a prison cell when you can witness MY glorious conquering of this pathetic planet firsthand!

My indestructible—and I might add quite handsome—army of Uncanny CanBots stands ready in my underground lair to unleash havoc across the globe! I merely have to give the order, sit back in my tree house lair, and wait for the planet to surrender!

What that ridiculous relic of a Supervillain could not accomplish in his entire career, I will achieve in my very first week of existence! I shall unleash a thunderous storm of indescribable villainy the likes of which this planet has never seen! The earth and everything and everyone on it will be reduced to mere playthings for me to do with as I please! And I shall rule with the iron fist of supreme evilosity! MUAHAHAHAHA!!!

CHAPTER FOURTEEN

Thirty years from now . . .

Having overcome the destruction of his indestructible
CanBot army some three decades earlier . . .

... the Supervillain formerly known as "Vordy" carefully tightens the final shackle securing his arch-nemesis, Captain Virtue, to the diabolically clever death trap.

Captain Virtue is the Superheroic son of Commander Virtue, who a previous, inferior Vordak the Incomprehensible had failed to dispose of—even though he had captured HIS Virtue no fewer than thirty-seven separate times.

This new—and quite obviously improved—Vordak the Incomprehensible learned much from his failed predecessor. **His** diabolical death traps are fast-moving.

Captain Virtue represents the final obstacle between *this* Vordak and his nefarious Evil Plan to RULE THE WORLD!

Before moving the trap's lever to the ON position, Vordak takes a few moments to reveal the details of his Evil Plan to his helpless arch-nemesis and to mock the safely secured Superhero for his failure to thwart him.

Virtue motions Vordak to come closer.
He clearly has very little strength remaining,
yet desperately wishes to whisper something
to his mighty vanquisher.

Vordak leans in close.
Using every ounce of
energy he can muster,
the defeated Superhero
raises his head to meet
Vordak, slowly parts his
lips, and . . .

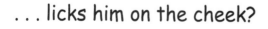

. . . licks him on the cheek?

GREAT GARGLING GHOSTS, Cataclysm! How many times have I told you not to wake me when I'm asleep on the sofa?!

MEANWHILE . . .
deep within the confines of a
top secret, evil location . . .

"Hey! who is that?"

What? Don't you get it? I cleverly cloned myself before allowing Commander Virtue to take "me" away to prison thirty years ago! Did you even *look* at page 163?! Did you *bother* to carefully consider every diabolical detail on page 167?! GREAT GASSY GOBLINS—I need a nap!

AMAZING!

INCREDIBLE!

ASTONISHING!

HANDSOME!

NEATO!

TURN THE PAGE!

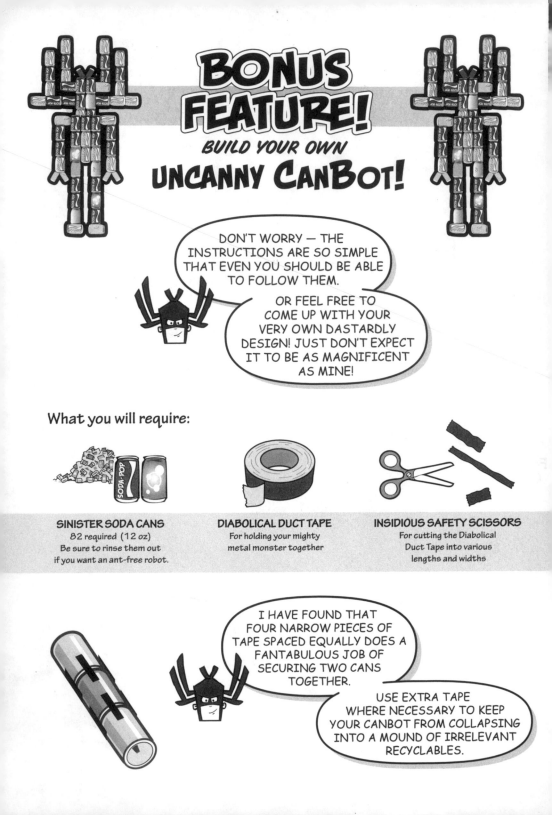

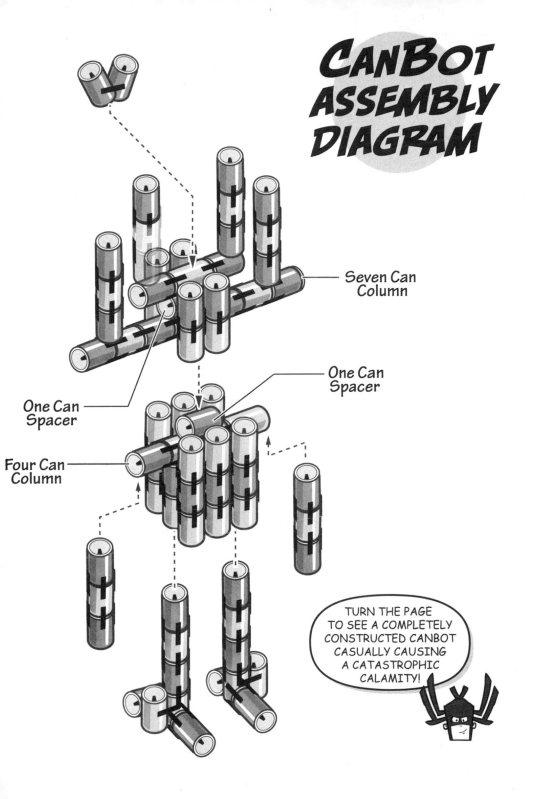

CANBOT
ASSEMBLY
DIAGRAM

Seven Can
Column

One Can
Spacer

One Can
Spacer

Four Can
Column

TURN THE PAGE
TO SEE A COMPLETELY
CONSTRUCTED CANBOT
CASUALLY CAUSING
A CATASTROPHIC
CALAMITY!

ABOUT THE AUTHOR

VORDAK THE INCOMPREHENSIBLE is a world-class Supervillain and the Evil Master of all he surveys. His first two books, *Vordak the Incomprehensible: How to Grow Up and Rule the World* and *Rule The School* have inspired a whole new generation of minions and fiends. His current whereabouts are unknown. You are hereby instructed to visit Vordak online at www.vordak.com, and he will know if you don't, so beware.

ABOUT THE MINIONS

SCOTT SEEGERT was selected to transcribe Vordak's notes based on his ability to be easily captured. He has completely forgotten what fresh air smells like and has learned to subsist on a diet of beetles, shackle rust, and scabs. As far as he knows, he still has a wife and three children in southeast Michigan.

JOHN MARTIN had the great misfortune of being chosen by Vordak to illustrate this book. He hasn't seen the sun in years and spends his free time counting down the months to his annual change of underwear. The last he heard, he also had a wife and three children living in southeast Michigan.

OTHER BOOKS BY VORDAK THE INCOMPREHENSIBLE